David stared at the woman in the doorway.

Her eyes were flashing fire.

Her mouth, which no doubt would be described as lush by advertising standards, had a disapproving downturn.

And she was wearing one of those power suits, dark and businesslike, with a flash of hot-pink silk teasing suggestively at the neckline.

He doubted she recognized the provocative effect. She struck him as the type who would have disapproved of it. He completed his survey and decided she was the kind of woman he genuinely disliked.

"Who the hell are you?" he demanded.

She ignored his tone and withdrew a legal document. "Mr. Winthrop," she said, "your son would like to file for a divorce."

She waited just long enough for that incredible piece of news to sink in, then added, "From you."

Dear Reader,

Welcome to Silhouette **Special Edition** . . . welcome to romance.

Last year, I requested your opinions on the books that we publish. Thank you for the many thoughtful comments. For the next couple of months, I'd like to share quotes with you from those letters. This seems very appropriate while we are in the midst of the THAT SPECIAL WOMAN! promotion. Each one of our readers is a *special* woman, as heroic as the heroines in our books.

Our THAT SPECIAL WOMAN! title for this month is *Kate's Vow,* by Sherryl Woods. You may remember Kate from Sherryl's VOWS trilogy. Kate has taken on a new client—and the verdict is love!

July is full of heat with *The Rogue* by Lindsay McKenna. This book continues her new series, MORGAN'S MERCENARIES. Also in store is Laurie Paige's *Home for a Wild Heart*—the first book of her WILD RIVER TRILOGY. And wrapping up this month of fireworks are books from other favorite authors: Christine Flynn, Celeste Hamilton and Bay Matthews!

I hope you enjoy this book, and all of the stories to come!

Sincerely,

Tara Gavin
Senior Editor

Quote of the Month: "I enjoy a well-thought-out romance. I enjoy complex issues—dealing with several perceptions of one situation. When I was young, romances taught me how to ask to be treated—what type of goals I could set my sights on. They really were my model for healthy relationships. The concept of not being able to judge 'Mr. Right' by first impressions helped me to find my husband, and the image of a strong woman helped me to stay strong."   —L. Montgomery, Connecticut

SHERRYL WOODS

KATE'S VOW

SPECIAL EDITION®

Published by Silhouette Books New York
America's Publisher of Contemporary Romance

SILHOUETTE BOOKS
300 East 42nd St., New York, N.Y. 10017

KATE'S VOW

Copyright © 1993 by Sherryl Woods

All rights reserved. Except for use in any review, the reproduction
or utilization of this work in whole or in part in any form by any
electronic, mechanical or other means, now known or hereafter
invented, including xerography, photocopying and recording, or in
any information storage or retrieval system, is forbidden without
the permission of the publisher, Silhouette Books, 300 E. 42nd St.,
New York, N.Y. 10017

ISBN: 0-373-09823-5

First Silhouette Books printing July 1993

All the characters in this book have no existence outside the
imagination of the author and have no relation whatsoever to
anyone bearing the same name or names. They are not even
distantly inspired by any individual known or unknown to the
author, and all incidents are pure invention.

®: Trademark used under license and registered in the United States
Patent and Trademark Office and in other countries.

Printed in the U.S.A.

SHERRYL WOODS

lives by the ocean, which, she says, provides daily inspiration for the romance in her soul. She further explains that her years as a television critic taught her about steamy plots and humor; her years as a travel editor took her to exotic locations; and her years as a crummy weekend tennis player taught her to stick with what she enjoyed most—writing. "What better way is there," Sherryl asks, "to combine all that experience than by creating romantic stories?"

Elizabeth Newton Halloran
requests the pleasure of
your company
as Kate Newton
and
David Allen Winthrop II
exchange their wedding vows
at eleven o'clock in the morning
on the fourteenth of November
at the Wayfarer's Chapel,
Pacific Coast Highway,
Palos Verdes, California

Chapter One

One more hour of paperwork, Kate Newton thought wearily. One more hour and this horrible week with its endless confrontations and sad, bitter stories of marriages gone wrong would be over. By Friday afternoons, what had once seemed challenging had lately become draining. It seemed she could hardly wait anymore to leave the office behind. That in itself was more troublesome than she cared to admit. High-priced, barracuda divorce attorneys were supposed to thrive on a steady diet of late hours and endless work. And until recently Kate had reveled in every minute of it.

She sighed as she stared at the piles of depositions and court documents still on her desk. She was suddenly struck by an unprofessional and almost irresistible urge to shake a few of her clients and tell them to wise up, drop their divorce petitions and fight for their marriages. Just the thought of doing something so completely out of character shook her. What the devil was wrong with her lately?

The buzz of her intercom provided an almost welcome interruption of her introspection, even though at this hour on a Friday it almost certainly promised disaster.

"Yes, Zelda," she said to her secretary, whose mother had been fascinated by F. Scott Fitzgerald and his flamboyant, nutty wife. Zelda Lane had taken the whole Fitzgerald mystique to heart and was every bit as colorful as her namesake. She was also, thank goodness, incredibly efficient.

"There's someone here to see you," Zelda said. Her voice dropped to a whisper. "He says he's a prospective client."

Something in Zelda's tone put Kate on alert. "Okay, what's the deal?" she asked irritably. "I don't have any appointments on my calendar. Is this one of those arrogant sons-of-bitches who expects to barge in and get first-class treatment?"

Her secretary uttered a sound that might have been a muffled hoot of laughter. "I don't think so, boss. I think this is one you ought to see."

Kate sighed. Unfortunately Zelda's instincts were usually worth exploring. "Does this prospective client have a name?"

"David Allen Winthrop," she said.

Kate heard a muffled exchange, then Zelda added, "The third. David Allen Winthrop III."

Kate knew all about men who were so precise, so full of themselves and their own importance. They were the kind she normally preferred to take to the cleaners in a divorce proceeding.

"Send him in," she said, already plotting her strategy for putting the bozo in his place with a stern lecture on busy schedules and the courtesy of making appointments.

Her office door swung open to admit the red-headed Zelda, whose expression hovered between amusement and anticipation. In a woman with her zany, off-beat sense of humor, that was yet another warning signal. Kate should have slammed the door on her secretary and the as-yet-unseen prospective client, sneaked out the back door and headed for a long weekend of much-needed relaxation in Malibu.

She watched the doorway expectantly, her gaze leveled just above Zelda's shoulder. The movement she saw, however, was waist high. She glanced down. Her mouth dropped open in astonishment. Her would-be client was about ten years old.

She blinked at the kid, whose sandy hair had been slicked back neatly. His face, with its smattering of freckles across the nose, had been scrubbed clean. His gray blazer and navy slacks looked as if they had come off the junior rack at Brooks Brothers. The stylish effect was completed by a perfectly knotted tie and a white dress shirt. Either this kid's summer camp had a rigid dress code or he was practicing for Wall Street at a very early age.

Judging from his earnest expression that whatever had brought him here was deadly serious to him, Kate held out her hand and formally introduced herself. "I'm Kate Newton, Mr. Winthrop. What can I do for you?"

Huge brown eyes regarded her somberly. "I'd like a divorce." He said it in the same unemotional tone with which he might order vanilla ice cream, even though everyone knew he'd really prefer chocolate.

Kate's composure slipped a notch. "Excuse me?"

Uncertainty flickered in his eyes for just an instant. "That's what you do, isn't it? You handle divorces?" His voice began to regain a little of his earlier confidence. "I read all about your last case in the paper. It sounded like you were good. A little rough on the husband, but generally quite good."

Kate was struck by the unexpected insightfulness from a pint-size analyst who should have been playing *zap-bang* computer games.

"Thank you, but I'm afraid I don't quite understand. You seem—" She fumbled for a word that wouldn't offend his determined dignity. She settled for blunt. "It's just that most people who get a divorce are a little older. Who exactly do you want to divorce?"

If this kid was married, she was giving up law, moving to a ranch in Montana and raising sheep. She wanted nothing further to do with the human race.

"My father," he said.

His tone was filled with such regret that Kate felt something deep inside her shift. Maternal instincts she'd never known she possessed roared to life. "I think we'd better talk, Mr. Winthrop. Why don't you have a seat over there on the sofa? How did you get here, by the way?"

"I'm supposed to be at a movie. Our housekeeper will pick me up."

Kate followed him to the conference area in her office and took a chair across from him. "Okay, then, why do you want to break things off with your father?" She absolutely refused to use the word divorce again.

"Irreconcilable differences," he said in that formal tone that gave Kate the creeps.

"I see." She nodded sagely and tried once more to gather her composure. Zelda's expression of barely controlled mirth wasn't helping. She glared at the secretary. "You can leave us now."

"Sure, boss. Could I bring you something? A soft drink, perhaps?" she said to the boy with as much deference as she would display toward an heiress. Zelda had had lots of practice with heiresses, but none that Kate was aware of with kids.

"Coffee," he told her, then added as if it was an afterthought, "with a lot of cream, please. And three sugars."

Kate, who drank her special-blend Columbian coffee black to savor the taste and aroma, cringed. Still, she couldn't help admiring a kid who was so determined to present a mature impression. Impression, hell, she corrected. This boy was more polite than half the men she knew. He was sitting soldier-straight on her sofa, even though the position looked awkward. His feet didn't quite reach the floor. There was none of the fidgeting that had driven her crazy with all of her sister's kids. The kid was so self-possessed, it was downright disconcerting.

When Zelda had delivered the coffee, Kate regarded her prospective client soberly. "Okay, why don't you tell me what this is all about?"

"I think it's fairly straightforward," he said, as if he'd been studying court documents for the proper wording. "My father and I don't get along."

"In what way?" she asked, genuinely fascinated now by both his demeanor and his claim. What would send a boy to a divorce attorney? Insufficient allowance? Strict discipline? A parental drug problem? Abuse? God forbid it was the latter.

"We never see each other anymore," he said, and then his lower lip trembled dangerously. "Not since my mom died."

Kate swallowed hard against the unexpected lump that formed in her throat. It was at least the size of a boulder. Her associates would be astounded at the rare display of emotion in a woman with a reputation for going for the jugular no matter how many tears were shed in the courtroom.

"When did your mom die?" she asked gently when she could form the words.

"Six months ago. It's been very hard on my dad," he said as if he'd heard that said by a zillion adults making excuses for a thoughtless parent.

"I'll bet it's been hard on you, too."

Those huge brown eyes, suddenly brimming with unshed tears, met hers. "Sometimes," he admitted in little more than a shaky whisper. A tear spilled down his cheek. "But I'm trying really hard to be brave for my dad's sake."

"Do you and your dad talk about it?"

He shook his head. "It makes us both too sad."

Kate suddenly wanted to leave her Century City office, go straight into Beverly Hills or Bel Air or whatever upscale part of town this man lived in and strangle him. No doubt he was hurting. Even without knowing the details of Mrs. Winthrop's death, she could imagine how devastating it must have been for her husband. She must have been very young, and that was never easy on anyone. But he had a son—a son who, for all his grown-up pretenses, was still a little boy who was hurting desperately inside. Kate recognized that kind of pain. She was at a complete loss about how to deal with it. The one thing she did know was that David Winthrop's way wasn't it.

"What would you do if you got a divorce?" she asked.

For only the second time since his unscheduled arrival, he appeared uncertain. "I was hoping maybe you could find someone who might adopt me. Maybe with some brothers and sisters, a mom and dad. You know, like a real family," he said wistfully. "Do you think you could find anyone like that? I wouldn't be any trouble. I promise.''

"Maybe it won't come to that," Kate said as a furious determination swept through her. David Allen Winthrop, Jr. or the second or whatever the hell this boy's father called himself was about to get hit with both barrels of her mighty indignation. She would make him feel like slime. She would negotiate a settlement for his precocious, lonely son, if it took a hundred hours of her extremely well-paid time. Pro bono. No charge. The mother and brothers and sisters were beyond her control, but by the time she was done, David would have his father back, she thought resolutely.

She held out her hand. "I will be happy to represent you," she said as she formally shook his hand. She was already thinking of a precedent-setting case recently in Florida that might provide her with ammunition.

Now that the deal had been struck, however, Davey looked uneasy. "You have to tell me about your fee first," he said. "I know you're probably expensive, but I have an allowance. I don't spend much of it. I have fifty dollars saved now. Is that enough, at least to start?" He held out some crumpled bills. A few pennies trickled to the floor, indicating the savings had been stashed in a piggy bank.

Kate extracted one dollar from the bills. "This is enough to put me on retainer," she said, refusing to hurt his pride by declining any payment at all. "I'll have Zelda give you a form to sign, saying you want me to be your lawyer. That will make everything official."

He looked doubtful. "You got a lot of money in that case I read about."

"It was a percentage of the settlement. We can make the same arrangement, if you like."

"You mean my dad would have to give you money when I get the divorce?"

"Something like that."

"He won't like that."

"They never do," Kate said dryly. "But the court will see to it."

In this case there would be no court and no settlement, if she had anything to say about it. In fact, she figured one stern lecture and some healthy outrage ought to fix things right up. Surely the boy's father wasn't being intentionally cruel. He was probably just a little misguided. Misguided could be straightened out in no time. It usually required no more than a determined logical assault.

"I'm very proud that you chose me to represent you," Kate said. "I will be in touch. I promise." She picked up one of her cards and scribbled on the back. "Take this. If you need me, call. I've given you my home number and my car phone."

He tucked the card carefully in his pocket. His already grave expression grew even more worried. "Will it take long? School starts soon, and if I'm going to have to go to a different one, I'd like to start with everyone else."

"I'm hoping it won't take long at all. You give Zelda your dad's address at work and your phone number at home. I'll get started today."

He hesitated at the door. "What if he gets mad and kicks me out before you can find anybody to adopt me?"

"You don't need to worry about that," she promised.

"But he might," he said, as if this man he obviously adored was likely to turn out to be a tyrant.

Kate didn't believe that for an instant, but she could see that he was genuinely worried about the prospect. With a rare impulsiveness she told him, "If he tries, you can stay with me until this is resolved."

His eyes brightened for the first time. "Do you have any kids?" he asked hopefully.

"No." It was something she'd never really regretted until now. At this moment she wished with all her heart that she could wave a magic wand and provide this kid with a ready-made family.

"Don't you have to ask your husband?"

The ingenuous question made Kate's hackles rise, but she merely shook her head. "No."

"Then that'd be okay, I guess."

In the last few minutes Kate had discovered that her dream child, one that skipped over all the messy stages, wasn't nearly as appealing as she'd thought. David Winthrop personified such a miniature adult. Yet she found that she wanted badly to reach out and muss his hair and tug that tie loose until he looked more like a carefree kid. She wanted to see him smile and to hear him laugh. She wanted to hug him and tell him that everything was going to be okay.

Even so, she held back. She had a feeling David Allen Winthrop, for all his self-possession, was holding himself together by a thread. She would do nothing that might offend the pride and dignity he wore like a protective cloak.

One thing was for certain—she'd never felt such a gut-deep need to make a case turn out right.

"Go home," Dorothy Paul told David Winthrop, scowling ferociously. Her plump, naturally cheerful face softened the impact of the scowl.

"It is Friday night," she reminded him. "The weekend is just beginning. Enjoy it. Go to the beach. Take your son to Disneyland. Go to a ball game."

"Are you through?" David asked, frowning back in annoyance. Obviously he'd given his assistant too much latitude. She thought she had the right to pry like some self-assigned mother hen.

"No, I am not through," she said, ignoring his exasperation. "You're working too hard. You have been ever since Alicia died."

"That's enough!" he snapped. The mere mention of Alicia's name brought back too many painful memories of those last days and weeks before her death. He couldn't relive that time. That was one of the reasons he slept fitfully, usually on the couch in his office. If he allowed himself to crawl back into the bed they had once shared so joyfully, he had unbearable nightmares about her suffering.

His longtime assistant regarded him patiently. "See what I mean? You would never use that tone with me if you weren't exhausted."

"I am using that tone with you because I am rapidly losing my temper."

To his regret, the look she shot him was full of pity, not fear. "David," she began in that gentle, mothering tone that was always a prelude to a lecture.

"Not tonight, Dorothy. Please. I'm beat."

"So, go home."

"I can't. I want to finish this one last sketch for the set for *Future Rock.*"

"What makes you think you know what Mars actually looks like?" she said, coming close to peer over his shoulder.

"I don't, at least not from personal experience," he countered. "But neither do you, so my guess is as good as anyone's."

"How many movie set designs have you worked on in the last six months?" She didn't wait for his reply. "I'll tell you. Four. That's more than you did in the past two years."

"I'm building a reputation. I'm in demand. You should be grateful. It allows me to pay you an exorbitant salary to keep this office running smoothly."

"You're hiding."

"Dorothy!"

To his deep regret, she ignored the warning note in his voice. "I will not shut up. I have watched you hiding out in this office long enough. It's time to start living again. If not for your sake, then think of Davey."

David ran his fingers through his hair. "Look, I know you mean well, but I have to handle this the best way I know how."

"By working yourself into a state of exhaustion? By ignoring your son?" she said.

"I couldn't have said it better myself."

The unfamiliar feminine voice, filled with derision, cut into their conversation.

Startled, David turned to stare at the slender, dark-haired woman standing in the doorway. Her wide-set eyes were flashing fire. Her mouth, which no doubt would be described as lush by advertising standards, had taken a disapproving downturn. She was wearing one of those power suits, dark and businesslike. A flash of hot pink silk at the neckline teased suggestively. He doubted she realized the provocative effect. She struck him as the type who would have disapproved of it.

He completed his survey and decided there wasn't a hint of vulnerability to soften all those hard edges. All in all, she was the kind of woman he genuinely disliked on sight. The exact opposite of Alicia, who'd been warm and gentle and compassionate, all soft curves and femininity.

"Who the hell are you?" he demanded ungraciously. "We're closed."

"Then you should have locked the door," she shot right back, clearly unintimidated by his lack of welcome.

He headed for the door to the workroom. "Dorothy, take care of this. I'll be in back," he said, retreating from the woman and from the unsettling effect she was having on him.

The woman looked ready to leap into his path. Dorothy, damn her, was practically racing for the opposite door.

"See you," his assistant said. "Like you said, we're closed. It's the weekend and I'm out of here."

"You're fired."

She beamed at him. "In that case, don't forget to clean the coffeepot before you go. You know how you hate it when it gets all cruddy after sitting all weekend."

Poised in midflight, David stared after his traitorous assistant. Then he regarded the unexpected visitor suspiciously.

"Are you a reporter?" There had been a lot of them lately, trying to sneak an advance look at the designs for *Future Rock,* which was being touted as the most ambitious futuristic drama since the advent of all the *Star Wars* films.

"No."

"If you're looking for a job, I don't have any available. Dorothy handles everything around here."

"Then I don't envy her," the woman retorted sympathetically.

David dealt with snippy, feminist women like this all the time, women who'd had to claw their way to the top of a sexist entertainment industry. Normally he gave as good as he got. Today he was simply too worn-out to try.

"Lady, obviously you have some sort of ax to grind," he said wearily. "Get it off your chest and leave me alone. I have work to do."

"Don't we all," she countered. "I'll bet mine is less pleasant than yours."

"Then I suggest you get it over with and leave us both in peace."

An odd expression, mostly anger, but touched by sadness, flashed across her face then. David suddenly began to wonder if it was going to be so easy to find peace again, once she'd said whatever was on her mind. He was bothered by a nagging memory of what she'd said when she walked into his office. It had been something that suggested she knew more about him than a stranger should. A reference to Davey?

"I'm here representing your son," she said.

The statement confirmed his recollection but added a startling twist. "My son," he repeated weakly. Then in a rush, he demanded, "Is Davey okay? What the hell do you mean you're representing him?"

She ignored his tone and slowly withdrew a piece of paper that for all the world looked like a legal document. She held it out. Heart thumping, he snatched it from her grasp. When he'd read it through, he regarded her in astonishment. As indignation washed through him, he waved the paper in her face.

"This says that my son has retained you as his legal counsel."

"Good. You can read. That will make things easier."

The cutting remark sailed right past him as he tried to focus on the meaning of the legal document in his hand. He finally met her gaze again, indignation suddenly tempered by genuine bewilderment. "He's a ten-year-old boy, for God's sake. What does he need a lawyer for?"

"Because, Mr. Winthrop, your son would like to file for a divorce." She waited just long enough for that incredible piece of news to sink in, then added, "From you."

Chapter Two

David couldn't have been more stunned if someone had told him that his futuristic sets, all products of a vivid imagination, were accurate depictions of far-off planets down to the last alien being and barren detail. He also felt a powerful surge of helplessness and anger that a total stranger knew more about what was going on in his son's head than he did. Why in God's name hadn't he seen this coming?

Of course, he consoled himself, it was entirely possible that this woman was making the whole charade up. He clung to that premise because it allowed him to retort with a heavy dose of sarcasm.

"You know, lady, I've heard of ambulance chasers in your business, but taking advantage of a ten-year-old boy is outrageous. I could have you brought up on charges.''

She didn't bat an eye. He had to admit that impressed him. And worried him.

"What charges?" she inquired with disconcerting calm. "I'm looking after my client's interests. Last I heard, that was what lawyers get paid to do."

"Paid? Now we're getting down to it, aren't we?" he said, almost sorry that this woman was the low-down vulture he'd first predicted her to be. "What's it going to take to get you off your high horse and out of my life? Name your price."

The derisive question brought a furious spark to those incredible, vivid eyes that were the shade of whisky shot through with fire. He couldn't seem to look away, fascinated despite himself by the immediate, passionate response that was evident before she said a word.

"How dare you!" she said, stepping up until they were toe to toe. In her high-heeled pumps, with her chin tilted up defiantly, their eyes were almost level.

"This isn't about money," she said slowly and emphatically, as if she wasn't entirely sure he could grasp plain English. "It isn't about me taking advantage of anyone. It's about a little boy's relationship with his father and, frankly, Mr. Winthrop, I'm beginning to see why he wants out."

Noble words, spoken with conviction. Hurled smack in his face, in fact. David recognized the technique. She was invading his space, trying to intimidate him. She was probably a real hellion in a courtroom, he thought with surprising admiration. Perhaps elsewhere, as well. A little shiver of awareness cut through his own outrage. Analyzing that unexpected reaction kept him from listening too closely to the accusations she was leveling at him, until one snagged his attention.

"...and neglect."

Neglect? He simply stared at her. "I do not neglect my son," he said in a low, furious tone that matched hers for righteous indignation. "He is fed and clothed. He has every toy, every opportunity a boy his age could possibly dream about. He's got more computer games than FAO Schwartz. He plays baseball, football and soccer. He has an Olympic-size pool in the backyard. If he expresses an interest in anything, he's signed up for lessons. Our housekeeper spends more time driving him around town than she does taking care of the house. He goes to the best private school in all of Los Angeles."

"I'm delighted your housekeeper is so dutiful. But frankly, for all the attention you've been paying him yourself, I'm surprised you don't have him in boarding school," she snapped back, clearly unimpressed by everything that had come before.

He cringed at that. He actually had considered boarding school at one point during Alicia's illness, but she had protested vehemently, had made him promise that Davey would never be sent away from home. He regarded this woman—Kate Newton, according to the paper she'd handed him—as if she were some sort of witch for having zeroed in on his single biggest weakness as a parent, his desire to deal with his anguish in his own time, in his own way...alone. And his ardent wish to spare his son from having to cope with one single instant of his own dark depression.

"I think you'd better go now," he said with quiet resolve, refusing to give in to his desire to shout at the top of his lungs. There was a tremendous temptation to take out months of pent-up frustration and grief on a woman he'd just met, because she was tearing open all of the raw wounds that time had not yet healed. He gestured toward the door. "You can show yourself out, I'm sure." He started for the workroom in back.

"We're not through," she retorted, staying right where she was. The low, natural command in her voice halted him in his tracks.

He turned slowly to face her. "I think we are, Ms. Newton. I've heard just about enough of your outlandish accusations. This business about representing a ten-year-old in a divorce proceeding against a parent is garbage. Any court in the country would laugh you out the door."

"Sorry. A child in Orlando won in a similar case just last fall. I'm surprised you didn't read about it. It was in all the papers." She glanced around, apparently taking in the elaborate, futuristic sketches pinned to the corkboard walls for the first time. "Of course, perhaps you don't live in the real world with the rest of us."

"So that's it," he said, finally beginning to get a glimmer of understanding about what had driven this woman to charge into his office like an avenging angel. If it wasn't money, then it had to be publicity. In the long run, one well-placed story in the Los Angeles paper and picked up by the wire services and networks would equal money in the bank.

He shook his head in disgust. "God knows how you zeroed in on Davey, but you probably took some innocent remark he made and latched on to it because you knew the case would generate a lot of publicity. Are you that desperate to get your career off the ground?"

Instead of lashing back with the fury he'd half expected, she simply laughed. To his bewilderment, the amusement seemed genuine. And the sound of that laughter did astonishing things to his pulse rate, stirred it in a way that all that yelling had not.

"Mister, I don't need the publicity," she retorted bluntly. "I get more than my share. That's how your son chose me. He read about my last case in the paper. As for the validity of the agreement David and I have, you have the retainer he signed. I think under the circumstances it would hold up in court." She shrugged. "But if that's not good enough for you, go home and ask him what he wants, ask him why he felt the need to retain a lawyer in the first place. At least, that's one way to assure that the two of you actually sit down and have a long-overdue conversation."

The sarcastic barb hit home, just as she'd obviously intended. Suddenly filled with despair as he realized that this situation wasn't going to evaporate, that she genuinely believed she was in the right, he felt all the fight drain out of him. "You're really serious about all this, aren't you?" he asked wearily.

"You bet I am. I don't like seeing a kid sitting in my office telling me that he and his father have quote, irreconcilable differences, unquote."

David sank down in a chair and regarded her miserably. "He said that?"

"That and a whole lot more," she retorted without a trace of sympathy. "It's been my experience, and Lord knows I've handled enough custody disputes, that kids don't make this sort of thing up. Even so, I'll give you the benefit of the doubt. Is there any truth to his claims? Have you been neglecting him? Shutting him out?"

He struggled with the answer to that one. "I suppose he might see things that way," he admitted eventually, not liking what that said about him as a father. He'd wanted desperately to believe that Davey didn't need him right now, because he wasn't at all sure he had anything left to give.

"Is there another way?" she asked. "What's your perspective?"

"My wife..." He couldn't even bring himself to complete the sentence aloud.

"Davey told me she died," she said, finishing it for him. She said it with the first hint of gentleness she'd displayed since storming into his office.

He regarded her in astonishment. "He actually told you that?"

"Does that surprise you?"

He nodded. "He never talks about it."

"He says it makes you both too sad."

The thought that Davey had recognized his anguish and shared that with this woman penetrated all the barriers he'd slid into place months before Alicia's death. To his amazement, he found himself saying more than he had to anyone in all these long weeks, the angry, tormented words spilling out before he could censor them.

"My wife's death was agonizingly slow and painful," he said. "It was horrifying to watch. It wasn't easy on any of us. I tried to protect Davey from the worst of it. So did Alicia. She insisted on being away from home, in a hospital, for the final weeks. Davey was only allowed to see her when she had her good spells. Those became increasingly infrequent."

"So even before she died, Davey already felt cut off from his mother," she said.

Phrased that way, it sounded like an accusation.

"We both felt it was best for him," David said stiffly.

"How do you protect a child from the fact that his mother is dying?" she asked quietly. "I still think about my father's last days. It's been years since he died and I was an adult when it happened, but I still remember his illness, how frightened I was at the prospect of losing him. I can't block out those thoughts because they might be painful. I know that eventually the good memories will begin to overshadow all the others. Why wouldn't Davey feel the same way?"

She paused for breath and regarded him evenly. "Why wouldn't you?"

David ignored the question because he had no answer for it. He was more fascinated by what she had just revealed about her own feelings. He had a hunch it was far more than she usually shared. He suspected that she, like he, tended to keep a tight grip on messy emotions. It struck him as all the more surprising, then, that she had taken Davey's side with such passion.

His impression of Kate Newton altered slightly. Perhaps she did really care about what happened to Davey, perhaps she was more capable of empathy than he'd given her credit for.

Then again, despite her disclaimers, perhaps she was simply meddling for the potential publicity a case with him at its center would generate. His might not be a household name, but the films he'd worked on were as familiar as those of Spielberg or Disney.

"Look, I appreciate your coming here and telling me about Davey," he said in an admittedly belated attempt to sound gracious and cooperative. "I'll have a talk with him. We'll work it out. Just send me the bill for your time."

She shook her head. "It doesn't work that way. Davey hired me. He has to fire me."

David felt his irritation climb again. Was there no getting rid of this pesky woman, even after he'd conceded that she'd made her point? "No document signed by a kid his age would be legal," he argued. "Drop it. You've done your job."

"I'm not referring to the legalities," she said stubbornly. "I'm discussing moral obligations. I took his case. I'll see it through."

He started to protest, but she cut him off. "I'm sure you mean well, Mr. Winthrop, but I have an obligation to my client. I hope you will talk to Davey. I hope you will work things out, but until he tells me the case is closed and he no longer wishes to divorce you, I'll be sticking around."

She stood up and headed for the door. David was about to breathe a sigh of relief, when she turned and faced him. She glanced pointedly at her watch. "It's nearly eight o'clock on a Friday night, Mr. Winthrop. If you meant what you said, shouldn't you be going home to your son?"

Kate thought the meeting had gone rather well. She'd served up a healthy combination of threats and guilt. With any luck David Allen Winthrop would take a good, hard look at himself and change his ways. He'd certainly looked shaken once he realized that she wasn't going to vanish without a fight, that she was taking his son's claims seriously.

Over the past ten years she had developed a keen eye for an adversary's weaknesses and strengths. As much as she'd been inclined to dislike him on sight, David Winthrop had struck her as a man who possessed a great deal of inner strength. He also was a man in pain. She had never known anyone who'd loved so deeply, whose grief was plainly written in the depths of his dark, almost midnight black eyes. Hopefully she had forced him to examine the price his son was paying while he struggled with his own suffering.

But she had meant what she'd said; she would be sticking to him like a burr until she was certain that her client had his father back again.

She was surprised by the shaft of anticipation that shot through her as she contemplated that prospect. When was the last time she'd even noticed a man in a sexual way? Months? A couple of years? She thought she'd pretty well buried her libido under a schedule that would wilt a well-trained athlete. The fact that she'd been at least marginally aware of David Winthrop's ruggedly handsome features and the snug fit of his jeans was downright startling.

That worrisome bit of self-awareness was still nagging at her when her car phone rang just as she turned onto Pacific Coast Highway heading up to her summer retreat in Malibu.

"Ms. Newton, this is Davey. You know, Davey Winthrop."

"Hi, Davey. What's up?" she asked, trying not to let on that she'd recognized the faint trace of fear in his voice. "Are you okay?"

"Yeah, I guess," he said, his voice flat.

"Davey, what's wrong?"

"I was just thinking, about the case and all. I think my dad is going to be really, really mad when he finds out. Maybe it would be a good idea if I came to live with you now."

She breathed a sigh of relief. So, that's all it was. Regret. She'd never met anyone seeking a divorce yet who didn't struggle with regrets the instant the decision had been made and the first steps taken. The calls came with such frequency that even Zelda had grown adept at all the necessary reassurances.

"Sweetheart, I just saw your father. I don't think he's mad at all." Except at me, she thought to herself. She probably should have crossed her fingers as she boldly lied. "In fact, I think he'll probably be home any minute and that things will start getting back to the way they used to be."

"Really?" Davey said, his voice suddenly filled with excitement. "You mean it?"

"I can't swear to it," she cautioned, "but I think so. Why don't you and I talk on Monday and see how the weekend went, okay?"

"Geez, yes," he said, sounding more like a high-spirited kid again. "I think I hear his car right now. 'Bye, Ms. Newton! Oh, yeah, thanks!"

As the phone thunked in her ear, Kate prayed she hadn't gotten his hopes set too high. If David Winthrop hurt that sweet, savvy kid again, he'd have to answer to her.

As David stepped out of the four-wheel-drive wagon that Alicia had insisted they needed to haul Davey and his friends around, his son came barreling through the front door. The huge, old Bel Air house had once belonged to some star of the silent-movie era, according to the real estate agent, who'd probably tacked an extra half a million on to the price for that bit of trivia. As overpriced as it had been, David had seen the glimmer of pleasure that a tie to the glamorous Hollywood past had put in Alicia's eyes, and he'd signed the papers without a second thought.

They had moved in six months before the cancer had been diagnosed. For those six months his wife had been deliriously happy redecorating, putting her personal stamp on every room.

David watched his son, and for an instant he could almost believe that Kate Newton's visit had been a bad dream. His son looked healthy, vital and every bit as exuberant as any other ten-year-old. Until he caught the shadows in his eyes. Then he knew that there was some measure of truth in what the attorney had told him, and his heart ached.

"Hi, Dad! Did you eat yet? Mrs. Larsen is fixing pot roast. She says it's almost ready." A worried frown creased his brow. "That's your favorite, isn't it? I told her it was. She said you might not get home in time for dinner and that everything would go to waste, but she made it anyway."

"Pot roast is definitely my favorite," David said, blinking hard against the tears that always threatened when he saw so many reminders of Alicia in his son. The same reddish blond hair, the same devilish brown eyes, the same scattering of freckles across his nose and that same crooked smile, flanked by dimples. Given what he now knew about Davey's sorrow, that hopeful, impish smile nearly broke his heart. "How was your day?"

The smile faltered slightly. "Okay, I guess," he said, looking guilty "I mot this lady today. I guess you know about that, huh?"

"Ms. Newton," David said, trying not to sound angry. How could he blame Davey for taking desperate measures? It was his fault his son had gone to see a lawyer.

"Yeah. She said she talked to you." Davey regarded him worriedly. "You're not mad, are you? I had to see her, Dad. I had to."

David hunkered down until they were eye to eye. "Are you so upset with me that you really want to leave home and find a new family?" David asked, unwilling to concede even to himself how much that hurt.

"I guess," Davey said, shifting from foot to foot uneasily.

"Why?"

Davey's expression suddenly turned belligerent. "You're never here anyway. It probably doesn't even matter to you what I do."

David sighed. "Oh, Davey," he said, his voice filled with regret. "It matters. I promise you, son. What you do will always matter to me. You're the most precious part of my life."

"Then how come you never spend any time with me?"

Months of hurt were obviously summed up in that one damning question. David found himself reacting as if he were under siege. "I do spend time with you," he countered too sharply.

Davy shook his head. "Not like you used to. You're always too busy. You haven't been to one single game all summer. Most of the time you're at the office. Even when you're here, it's like you don't even see me. You're always telling me to be quiet and stuff."

"Because I'm working. I have to earn a living," he said, fully aware of the defensive note that had crept into his voice but unable to contain it. Kate Newton had touched off a spark of guilt in him. Davey was fanning it into a roaring blaze.

"Yeah, I guess," Davey said, sounding defeated. He started for the stairs.

"Where are you going? I thought you said dinner was almost ready."

That steady gaze met his. "I don't think I'm very hungry anymore."

As David stared after him, his son plodded up the stairs as if he carried the weight of the world on his narrow shoulders.

Chapter Three

"So, boss, how'd it go with your new client?" Zelda inquired on Monday afternoon when Kate finally reached the office after a long, frustrating morning in court. Zelda grinned. "Filed his divorce papers yet?"

Already irritable, Kate wasn't amused by her secretary's lighthearted attitude. She put aside the stack of messages on her desk and scowled as she searched for the Winthrop file. "It's not a joke, Zelda. Not to me and certainly not to Davey."

Zelda looked hurt by the reprimand. "I know that. But you have to admit it's pretty unusual. You're not really going through with it, though, are you? He's just a kid. That Orlando case might have set a precedent, but I doubt the courts are going to start granting divorce decrees for disgruntled kids the way they do for adults."

"In some cases, they may be justified," Kate said, thinking of the way David Winthrop had deliberately distanced himself from his son. She wasn't at all convinced he could mend his ways, even if he genuinely wanted too. She'd never much believed in behavioral changes brought on by the threat of legal action, either. They seldom lasted past the final court date.

"You didn't like Davey's father much, did you?" Zelda guessed.

Kate didn't waste time reminding her that she wasn't the one who had to like David Winthrop. He was Davey's father and it was obvious the boy loved him. Her own reaction wasn't all that clear-cut. "You sound surprised," she said.

"It's just that I've read about his father. He sounded like an okay guy. He's some bigwig in the movies. I think he's even won an Oscar."

Kate glanced up from the notes she'd made after her meeting with David Winthrop. "He has? For what?"

Zelda shook her head in dismay. "For a woman born and raised in Hollywood, you don't know zip about the movie business, do you?"

"Who has time for movies? Just tell me. What does David Winthrop do?"

"Set design, sometimes on those comic-book action pictures, but mostly on the big sci-fi movies. His newest one has everyone in town talking. I think it's called *Future Rock*. Every reporter in town is trying to sneak a look at his sketches."

Kate recalled all the designs pinned to his office walls. "Oh, yeah, I guess that's what he was working on when I was there Friday night."

Zelda's turquoise eyes grew round. "You actually got into his office? You saw the designs?"

"I suppose," she said, unable to work up nearly as much excitement over those as she had over the unusually dark and mysterious color of the man's eyes. Still she made a mental note about David Winthrop's professional life. Surely the fantasy worlds he created would be fascinating to a ten-year-old boy. Perhaps those could provide a bridge between him and his son.

"So what'd they look like?" Zelda demanded, perching on the corner of her desk, her face alight with curiosity.

Kate shrugged. "I didn't pay much attention."

Zelda groaned. "Do you realize what it would do for my social life if I could say that I know someone who saw those designs?"

Kate chuckled. "Well, that much is true."

"Sure, but who'd believe me if I couldn't even describe one? Come on, boss, surely you can remember some little detail."

"Afraid not."

Disappointment washed across her secretary's face. "What's he like?" she asked finally. "I mean, really. Be objective."

Kate glanced up again. "Objective about what?"

"David Winthrop," Zelda said impatiently.

"He's…" She searched for a description that would satisfy Zelda's curiosity without stirring her overly active imagination. She didn't dare say anything about the way the man's temper had riled her. She couldn't mention that she'd been intrigued by the sorrow in the depths of his eyes. She settled for *pleasant*. To be honest, the description was far from accurate, but it was definitely innocuous enough to suit her purposes.

"Pleasant," Zelda repeated incredulously. "What does that mean? Dinner is pleasant. Mediocre movies are pleasant. Men are either fascinating or dull or out-and-out creeps."

Kate laughed. "Those are my only choices?"

"In my experience."

Zelda had vast amounts of experience, which she was willing to share in the form of anecdotes or advice. "Given that, I'd have to say fascinating," Kate conceded, thinking of the layers to David Winthrop that she'd suspected, but hadn't begun to plumb and probably never would.

Zelda's eyes lit up. "Okay, now we're getting somewhere. So you did like him, after all?"

"I didn't say that."

"Sure you did. No man has climbed beyond dull on your rating system for ages now."

Unfortunately Zelda's perceptiveness was sometimes a pain in the neck. So was her tendency to think that Kate's social life was fair game for discussion.

"Zelda, the man is our adversary. We represent his son."

"What does that have to do with whether or not he's a hunk?"

"I did not say he was a hunk," Kate protested.

"You said fascinating. That's close enough."

"Zelda, don't you have work to do?"

"Sure. I always have work to do," she said, not budging.

"Then go do it," Kate prodded.

"Oh," she said, her eyes blinking wide. "Sure." She made it as far as the door before she turned back. "It's a good thing your new stepfather doesn't know about this David Winthrop, huh?"

"What is that supposed to mean?" Kate demanded, though she knew perfectly well what Zelda was getting at. Brandon Halloran had taken a personal interest in her future not ten seconds after he and her mother had spoken their wedding vows. Given his meddling ways, Zelda was right on target. Brandon would latch on to the news of Kate's *fascination* with David Winthrop and start making plans for a wedding.

Kate's gaze narrowed. "He will not hear about this from you, will he?"

"Me?" she repeated innocently. "Never. Of course, the man does seem to have a real nose for romance. You told me how he plotted to marry off his grandson. I'd be real careful what you tell him about your current caseload."

"Brandon and I do not discuss my caseload. He and my mother are on their honeymoon. If we discuss anything at all, it's which European capital they intend to visit next."

"Oh, I guess he doesn't bother to ask you because he's already pumped me for all the information he wants," Zelda added slyly.

Kate's heart plummeted. "He what?"

"Don't worry, boss. I am very discreet."

Kate scowled at her. "See that you are or you will be very unemployed." The last thing she needed was Brandon Halloran taking an active interest in her love life. In fact, she didn't especially want her new step-father involved in any aspect of her life. She'd had a wonderful father she'd adored. She didn't need a replacement.

For the next three hours Kate returned urgent phone calls, delegating those less pressing to Zelda. At four-thirty, she packed up her briefcase and walked out of her office. "I'm gone for the day."

Zelda regarded her with open astonishment. "It's only four-thirty."

"I have to visit a client."

Her secretary glanced at the appointment book in front of her. "Which client? It's not in here. Boss, how do you ever expect the accountant to keep the billing straight if you forget to write things down on the calendar?"

"This isn't a billable appointment. I'm going to see Davey Winthrop."

Zelda propped her chin on her hand and contemplated her boss with a look that was openly speculative. "Oh, really?"

Kate glowered at her. "I'll check in for messages about six. Don't beep me unless it's an emergency."

"You got it. I don't suppose you're planning to have a cozy mediation meeting between father and son over a snack of milk and cookies?"

"No. I'm sure your hotshot set designer will still be in his office. I'm out of here. Call Davey and let him know I'm on my way."

She found him waiting on the front steps, wearing a neatly pressed cotton shirt and jeans with creases so sharp they could have sliced through butter at the very least. His expression was thoroughly dejected. The weekend had obviously not gone nearly as well as she'd hoped. She took a seat beside him.

"How you doing?" she asked.

"Okay," he said without looking up.

"How'd things go with your dad?"

He glanced at her then. "Not so good. I think he was mad at me for talking to you."

"What makes you say that?" she asked, infuriated by the thought that David Winthrop might have taken her visit out on his son.

"We started to talk when he got home Friday night, but then he got mad and then I got mad." He shrugged. "Nothing's changed. Not really. He acted like everything was all my fault. I think he's really mad about what I did. I knew he would be."

"He was probably more embarrassed than mad. Sometimes grown-ups don't want other people to know about their troubles."

"I guess."

"Did you do anything together?"

"Not really. He stayed at home, though. I guess he's trying."

Staying at home didn't sound like much to her. He obviously wasn't trying hard enough by Kate's standards. "Why don't you and I have dinner together?" she suggested impulsively. "Do you have plans?"

His expression brightened. "Really? You can stay?"

"Absolutely. We'll work out a settlement plan to propose to your dad. Will your housekeeper mind if you invite a guest?"

"Heck no. She always makes a ton of stuff anyway, just in case Dad comes home. He almost never does," he added forlornly.

Mrs. Larsen gave Kate a thorough once-over when Davey introduced them. The lines in her face suggested her mouth was always turned down in a perpetual frown. Still, she was polite enough when she was told that Kate had been invited to stay for dinner.

"I hope you don't mind," Kate said.

"There's plenty," Mrs. Larsen responded succinctly. She scowled at Davey. "Young man, have you washed your hands?" she demanded, hands on ample hips.

Davey grinned, not put off in the least by the older woman's brusque tone. "You ask me that every night."

"Because you never wash until I do," she retorted. "Now get along with you."

When Davey had gone, Kate asked, "Are you sure you don't mind my staying?"

"It'll be good for Davey to have company," the housekeeper said grudgingly. "The boy's alone too much. He eats in the kitchen with me most nights, but I'm afraid I'm not much company by that hour. I like to watch the news and, tell the truth, I'm pretty worn out after taking him this place and that all day long. I'm sixty-five. I don't have the stamina I once did."

Kate sensed this was the start of a familiar lament. "I'm sure a boy Davey's age is always on the go."

"Indeed," Mrs. Larsen said. "Summertime's the worst. It's hot as the dickens here in town, and the boy's into everything. In my day, a child's friends all lived in their neighborhood. Davey's are scattered all over the county." She shook her head, clearly disapproving of the changes in society.

"How do you think Davey and his father get along?" Kate ventured cautiously.

"I'm not one to gossip, miss," Mrs. Larsen replied sternly.

"I'm sure," Kate agreed. "But I am trying to help Davey. To do that I really need to know what you've observed. You're closer to the two of them than anyone."

The housekeeper appeared placated by the explanation. "That's true enough," she said. "I suppose since it's for Davey's sake, I could tell you what it seems like to me. I've been with the family since Davey was a toddler. The two of them adore each other. Always have. That's why it's been so sad, seeing how Mr. David spends all his time at the office these days. He claims it's because he's got more work than he can handle, but the truth of it is that he just can't bear to be in this house.''

''You mean since his wife died?''

Mrs. Larsen nodded. ''This place was Miss Alicia's choice. Her touch is on every room. I doubt he's admitted, even to himself, how much that bothers him. Asked him once why he didn't move after she was gone. He liked to bit my head off.'' She shook her head sorrowfully. ''I haven't said another word about it. He'll snap out of it one of these days. It'll just take time.''

''And in the meantime, Davey's suffering,'' Kate murmured, more to herself than the housekeeper.

When Davey came back and they were seated at one end of the huge, formal dining room table, Kate suggested they draft a schedule of the time Davey wanted his father to spend with him.

''And he'll have to do what I ask?''

''We'll negotiate,'' Kate explained. ''But yes, I think he'll agree to most of it.''

Breakfast every morning, he suggested, glancing at Kate for approval. She nodded and made a note. An hour each evening before bedtime. Saturday and Sunday afternoons. One all-day outing a month on a weekend. The requests seemed pitifully small and yet it was clear from the hopeful gleam in his eyes that they would mean so much to Davey.

As Kate drew up the list, she used her own childhood as a model, then modified that optimum to allow for David Winthrop's current emotional state. It would be pointless to demand that he correct everything overnight. If she could get him to commit to making small changes, the big ones would come eventually. Coaching one of those teams his son was on, perhaps. A weekend fishing trip. An honest-to-goodness vacation.

Kate thought back to the special relationship she had shared with her father. He had always been there for her and Ellen, cheering them on in sports, encouraging them with their schoolwork.

Only recently had she discovered that he hadn't even been Ellen's natural father. Yet he had never openly differentiated between the two of them. If Kate and he had shared a special bond, he had done his best to balance that by spending extra time with her sister. She couldn't imagine what life would have been like if he hadn't played such an integral role in their family.

To Kate's growing irritation, David Winthrop still wasn't home by Davey's bedtime. Mrs. Larsen found them in Davey's playroom, a huge, cheerful room filled with games, long-neglected stuffed animals, a rocking horse, sporting equipment and a state-of-the-art computer. The colorful storybook murals on the wall had obviously been painted with loving attention to detail. Davey had confirmed that his father had done them.

Mrs. Larsen observed Kate and Davey silently from the doorway for a moment before saying firmly, "Bedtime, young man."

"But I have company," he protested, glancing up from the Monopoly board. "Besides, Ms. Newton owes me a bundle. I've loaned her a lot of money and I'm about to foreclose on her last property."

Mrs. Larsen gave Kate an understanding look. "The boy's destined to be a real estate mogul."

"He's sneaky," Kate added. "Had me in hock up to my eyeballs before I realized what he was up to."

The housekeeper's mouth curved faintly in what probably passed for a smile. "Then it's definitely bedtime. We adults have to stick together. Davey, I'm sure Ms. Newton understands that rules are rules around here."

"I certainly do," Kate said with obvious gratitude.

Davey grinned. "You just don't like losing."

"Nope," Kate agreed. "Never have."

He regarded her hopefully. "Could you tuck me in? I don't really need anyone to do that," he added quickly. "But I thought maybe you'd want to, since you don't have any kids of your own."

Kate swallowed hard, touched by the bravado that masked a cry for affection. "I would be happy to tuck you in."

"I have to take a shower first, but I won't be long. You won't leave, will you?"

Kate cast a look at the usually stiff housekeeper and discovered that her eyes were surprisingly misty. Sensing no disapproval from that quarter, she shook her head. "I'll wait right here," she promised.

When Davey had gone, Mrs. Larsen regarded her somberly. "The boy misses his mother. What you're doing for him is a real nice thing," she said stiffly.

She walked out before Kate could respond. Kate wondered if she knew the real reason Kate was around or if she'd simply been referring to her agreement to remain to tuck the boy in.

When Davey came in a few minutes later, he was wearing pajamas, and his damp, sandy hair was slicked back. He showed Kate his room, pointing out pictures of his softball and soccer teams, the trophy he'd won for football. "We were champions," he told her as he smothered a yawn.

"I'll bet your dad was really proud," Kate said.

Davey shrugged. "I guess. He didn't get to the game. He had to work."

"Things like that happen sometimes," Kate told him, thinking of how many times she had put social engagements on hold because of a backlog of work. It wasn't the first time it had occurred to her that she might have been every bit as distracted from parental responsibilities as David Winthrop, and without the recent loss of a spouse as an excuse.

"I'm sure he wanted to be there," she said, mouthing the platitude in the faint hope that it would reassure Davey.

"He never even asked about it," Davey retorted, then sighed. "I guess he just forgot." He glanced at Kate. "Do you ever wish you had a kid like me?"

Kate felt an odd and definitely unexpected twinge of yearning deep inside. "Yes," she said. She meant it only to reassure him, but as she spoke she realized with amazement that it was true. Right this instant she did wish she had a child who cared whether she was home at night, a child who wanted desperately to share the excitement of accomplishments, a child who would give meaning to an existence that had recently seemed to lack focus.

She smoothed his hair and smiled as his eyelids fluttered closed. "Yes," she said again softly. "I wish that I had a boy just like you."

It was nearly one in the morning when David finally trudged wearily into the house. He'd meant to get home earlier, but somehow the work had been so engrossing that he'd never even noticed the time.

Who was he trying to kid? He hadn't been able to bear the thought of spending another night trying to figure out how to form a new bond with his son. The weekend had been sheer torture. Davey's patient, hopeful glances had filled him with an intolerable level of guilt and left him wishing that parenthood came with an instruction book. It had never seemed difficult when Alicia was alive. She had planned outings. She had been the driving force that had filled the big old house with laughter.

He walked into the den, tossed his jacket on the back of a chair and poured himself a drink. Only then did he notice Kate Newton, sound asleep in a wing chair in front of the French doors opening onto the patio.

He stood over her, indulging this odd fascination she seemed to hold for him. She was wearing another one of those power suits, this one in a pale gray. A ruffle of ice blue silk edged the deep V neckline. She had kicked off her gray high heels and sat with her legs tucked under her. A slight breeze fanned the cloud of black hair that fell in curling wisps against her cheek. For the first time since he'd met her, she looked utterly feminine and vulnerable. Desirable, he thought, recognizing the sharp awakening of his senses with amazement.

As if she'd been aware of the wayward direction of his thoughts, she snapped awake, blinked and immediately began hunting for her shoes. David grinned as she jammed her feet into them. Cinderella fearful of having to deal with a prince? He held up the decanter of brandy.

"Would you like a drink?"

She shook her head. He shrugged and poured his own, then sank down in the chair opposite her.

For a moment he simply relished the blessed silence and the unexpected, but surprisingly welcome companionship. Then finally, knowing that the topic couldn't be avoided forever, he asked, "What are you doing here?"

"I had a business dinner with my client."

He regarded her in disbelief. "You had dinner here, with Davey?"

"There was no one else around to eat with him," she said.

There was no mistaking the note of censure. "Mrs. Larsen is here," he retorted.

"I'm sure Mrs. Larsen is a lovely woman. I know she's a terrific cook. But she is sixty-five years old and she prefers to eat in the kitchen alone with the TV blaring.''

"How would you know that?''

"She told me herself.''

David sighed in defeat. "I don't know what you want me to do. I have a career.''

"No one's career takes that much time,'' she countered sharply.

Something in her voice alerted him that even she found a certain irony in that statement coming from her. "Not even yours, Ms. Newton?''

"I don't have a son at home who needs me.''

He regarded her curiously. "Who do you have waiting for you at the end of the day?''

"At the moment, my mother's cats. She's off on her honeymoon.''

"And as we all know, cats are pretty independent, so you can stay out as late as you want.''

"We're not talking about me, Mr. Winthrop.'' She reached for a piece of paper. "Davey and I drew up a list of ideas.''

"Demands.''

She shrugged. "Whatever. I think they're reasonable.''

David couldn't help being more intrigued than ever by the woman who was championing his son. He'd made a few calls over the weekend, checked her out and discovered that she had exactly the high-profile reputation she'd claimed. He'd also learned that she always represented the woman. He had a feeling there was a story behind that.

"How come you never take the man's side?" he asked, watching closely for her response.

"Because men usually have powerful allies in court, including a good many of the judges. I like to even the odds."

"Why'd you choose this kind of law? Were you getting even with some man who did a number on you?"

Though she didn't answer, he could see by her startled expression that he was right. "Who hurt you so badly, Kate Newton?" he asked. He'd formed the question first out of mild curiosity. Only after it was spoken did he suddenly realize that he genuinely wanted to know.

"It's an old story and hardly relevant," she said indifferently, though there was a faint flicker of pain in her eyes.

"If you're planning to meddle in my life, then I think everything about you is relevant."

"I wouldn't need to meddle if you'd just agree to the terms I've outlined."

He declined to accept the paper she held out. "I never deal with business matters this late. I like to look papers over carefully when I'm fully alert. In this case it would probably be a good idea to have my own lawyer examine them. Who knows what a woman with an ax to grind against men might try to do to entrap me," he said slyly. "Of course, if I knew a little more about you, perhaps that wouldn't be necessary."

She looked disconcerted by the subtle innuendo he'd allowed to underscore his taunt. "Another time," she said, plunking the paper on the table beside him and practically bolting for the door.

Surprised somehow by the skittish response, David followed at a more leisurely pace. "I'll hold you to that."

Outside, striding across a lawn already damp with dew, she slowed down just long enough to remind him, "I expect your response to our requests within the next few days."

"You'll have it tomorrow," he said, then, probably as much to his own amazement as to hers, he added impulsively, "Over dinner."

She halted in her tracks. Her gaze narrowed suspiciously. "With my client?"

David found himself grinning at discovering yet another flaw in that suit of armor she wore. Kate Newton might have the upper hand in a courtroom, but here, on his turf both literally and figuratively, he could clearly rattle her. He realized it delighted him in some indefinable way.

"If you insist," he said, making it an unmistakable taunt.

Clearly refusing to be daunted, she squared her shoulders. "I do, Mr. Winthrop. I most definitely do."

"Then, by all means, Ms. Newton. We will have our chaperon along."

He heard her indignant intake of breath as, chuckling, he turned and went back into the house. For some reason he felt better than he had in ages.

Chapter Four

Normally Kate spent her weeknights at her Century City apartment, only blocks from her office. The location saved transportation time, which was especially critical given the kind of jam-packed schedule she maintained. But after leaving David Winthrop, she was thoroughly wide-awake, far too wired to sleep.

Surely someone with her analytical capabilities could figure out why. It wasn't just the disturbing conversation they'd had before she'd left the house, she decided finally. It was the way she'd felt when she'd awakened to find him studying her so intently. There had been a cozy intimacy, a sweet tenderness to that moment that had struck a responsive chord somewhere deep inside her. Combine that with the way she'd felt when she'd kissed Davey good-night and she could be heading for emotional disaster.

In an attempt to derail herself from that track and to rid herself of that disconcerting sensation, she found herself driving the entire winding length of Sunset Boulevard, emerging finally on Pacific Coast Highway. She turned toward Malibu.

But as she drove along the dark coastal road, nearly deserted at this hour, she couldn't seem to shake the somewhat astonishing reaction she seemed to be having to David Winthrop and to his son. Was she suddenly going through some sort of mid-life crisis? True, her emotions had been topsy-turvy for weeks now, but this sudden maternal yearning and this unexpected awakening of her senses were so entirely out of character she had no idea what to make of them.

She knew all about marriages, the bad ones, anyway. By the time she met most couples, they were engaged in bitter acrimony, all positive aspects of their love wiped out by pain and anger.

By contrast, she'd always considered her own parents' marriage idyllic. Only recently had she discovered it had been more a marriage of convenience. She had been stunned by the revelation that while her father had adored her mother, her mother had secretly harbored a lifelong love for another man, Brandon Halloran. Worse, from Kate's perspective, her father had known about it, had accepted the bargain, willing to play second best to a memory.

All of that had only served to confirm her jaded view that even the best marriages represented nothing but a series of bad compromises. So, with every last illusion destroyed, why was she suddenly experiencing these faint stirrings of need to get involved in a relationship that could only lead to emptiness and pain?

Maybe it was a simple matter of lust, she consoled herself. She was a healthy, active woman whose hormones had been ignored for too long. Perhaps they were simply reminding her of that. And David Winthrop happened to be in the vicinity when the awakening occurred.

That had to be it. That was something she could understand. That was something she could control. She nodded in satisfaction as she parked in the garage of her modest Malibu beach house. She had no intention of indulging those wayward hormones, but it was good to know what she was battling here. She would be on her guard, especially around David Winthrop.

She winced as she recalled how easily he'd detected her motive for insisting that Davey join them for dinner. She might have protested for a month that her client had a perfect right to sit in on their meeting, but neither she nor David would have believed that was all there was to it. She wanted a chaperon, just as he'd accused in that amused tone of voice. And they both knew that the only reason she felt that way was because she was attracted to him and feared that attraction.

In the living room of the beach house, after opening the sliding glass doors to the pounding of the Pacific's surf, she dug through a stack of magazines she subscribed to mainly to have on hand for weekend guests. The most recent issues of a slick, monthly film magazine were buried amidst news weeklies, women's magazines and upscale architecture and gourmet periodicals. Kate flipped through, looking for any mention of David Winthrop or his set designs. Maybe she'd stumble across something that would cast him in such a negative light it would kill this stirring of fascination she felt.

She was skimming the last issue in the stack, one over a year old, when she turned a page and saw his face staring up at her. Eyes alight with excitement, he was standing in the interior of a comic-book world created for a blockbuster that had been released at Christmas. In his denim shirt and jeans, he looked every bit as handsome as the actor who'd played the superhero. In fact, she decided with careful objectivity, he was probably even more attractive with his natural, rugged masculinity, his careless hairstyle, the faint stubble of a beard on his cheeks. He appeared to be a man unaware of his looks, just confident in himself.

What struck her even more, though, was how alive he looked. Enthusiasm had chased away the shadows in his eyes. He seemed perfectly comfortable and happy in this make-believe world of primary colors and cartoon-style structures. It occurred to her, given the date of publication, that the picture had probably been shot before his wife's death, perhaps even before her illness had progressed to its terminal stages.

Kate touched her fingers to the laughing curve of his mouth and wondered if she would ever see this relaxed, lighthearted side of David Winthrop. She had a feeling if he was disturbing her equilibrium now with just a glimmer of his charm, he would be devastating if he ever turned the full force of that smile in her direction.

She was still holding the magazine when she finally fell into a restless, dream-filled sleep in which a larger-than-life hero bearing an uncanny resemblance to David Winthrop saved her from mythical dragons.

What the hell had he been thinking of? David wondered as the dinner hour approached on Tuesday night. The very last thing he wanted to do was have dinner with a woman whose avowed intention was to separate him from his son. Finding her in his living room in sleepy disarray the night before had momentarily blinded him to Kate Newton's real character.

After she'd gone, he'd looked over that damnable list she'd given him. Couched in legalese, it ordered him to adhere to a militaristic schedule of meetings with his son. He hadn't a doubt in the world that she intended to see that the timetable was enforced.

Dorothy poked her head into his office for their end-of-the-day consultation on the status of all his projects. "You're looking even grumpier than usual," she observed cheerfully as she came in and closed the door. "What's the problem?"

"Kate Newton is the problem," he complained without thinking.

"Who's Kate Newton?" Her eyes lit with sudden awareness. "I don't suppose she's that beauty who stormed in here on Friday night?"

He'd done it now. She'd pester him until she knew every last detail. "The same," he admitted, hoping that would be enough to satisfy her curiosity.

"You never did say what she wanted."

"No," he said pointedly. "I didn't."

Dorothy scowled at him. "I can't help if you clam up. Now who is she?"

"My son's lawyer."

Her eyes widened. "Uh-oh," she said, settling into a chair and putting aside the clipboard with its time-table for the various stages of the *Future Rock* set designs. "Let's hear it."

"Shouldn't we be going over that schedule?"

"In a minute. Now, talk."

David sighed and handed her the latest handwritten document with its list of demands for parental attention. Dorothy read it and nodded approvingly.

"So, what's the big deal?" she asked.

"The woman is trying to legislate my life."

"I've been trying to do that for years. You don't let me get under your skin. What's different about this woman? The fact that she's young and gorgeous and single, if the lack of a wedding ring is any indication?"

He regarded her in amazement. "You noticed whether or not she was wearing a ring?"

"I'm always on the lookout for single women for you. My goal in life is to see you happily involved again," she said complacently.

Those words, coming from a woman with Dorothy's determination, sent a shudder of dread through him. He decided she needed to understand that Kate Newton was not the woman for him.

"Did you even read that thing?" he demanded. "If I'm not careful, she'll be telling me which jobs to take."

"Maybe that would keep you from taking on too damn many," Dorothy shot right back. "Somebody has to slow you down. I'm certainly not getting through to you. And that agent of yours would have you working twenty-four hours a day just so his piece of the action would climb."

"Dammit, don't you see? She's trying to separate Davey and me."

"From the looks of this, I'd say the opposite is true," she countered in that logical, reasonable tone that made him want to chew nails. "David, all she's asking is that you spend more time with your son. What's so terrible about that? You and Davey used to spend all your spare time together. It's no wonder he's feeling neglected."

David sighed and rubbed his temples. His head was pounding. "I know," he admitted.

Dorothy regarded him curiously. "Are you sure there's not something more to your reaction? Are you feeling the slightest bit disloyal to Alicia because you're attracted to this woman?"

Leave it to Dorothy to nail it, he thought ruefully as he recalled the regrettably powerful and very masculine response he'd had to Kate Newton the night before. For one brief instant there, he'd actually found himself flirting with her. And enjoying it!

Almost the instant her car had pulled out of his driveway and he'd turned toward the house, he'd been weighed down by guilt. He'd vowed on the spot to call this morning and cancel the dinner invitation. He'd worked himself into a state over the paper Dorothy held, using indignation over that as an excuse for bowing out.

She regarded him sympathetically. "You're a widower. You have been for six months now. Being attracted to a woman is not a sin," Dorothy told him gently, obviously operating on the assumption that she'd guessed the truth. "Come on, boss. Alicia wouldn't want you to stop living. You know that. She'd want you to grab whatever happiness you can find."

Happiness in the form of Kate Newton, an attorney with ice in her veins? He struggled just a little with the concept. And yet, she definitely represented living. Everything about her suggested that she was vibrant and exciting and passionate, even if a little too driven and rigid for his taste. For a time she might make him feel alive. She might chase away the memories of death and mortality. But then what?

David sighed. "I know that's what Alicia would want," he said, agreeing bleakly with his assistant. "But sometimes living is just too damned painful."

The conversation with Dorothy had accomplished one thing, though. David decided against canceling the dinner with Kate and Davey. It would have been the cowardly way out and probably would have added ammunition she could use later, if she pursued this damnable divorce.

With his stomach tied in knots, he approached the informal restaurant she'd chosen in Century City. He blamed the upset on trepidation. The truth of the matter was, though, that it was probably anticipation that had him nervously pacing the outdoor mall as he watched for Kate and Davey to arrive. She had insisted on picking up his son, almost as if she feared he might exclude the boy at the last minute. The realization that she obviously felt she needed protection from him cheered him slightly. It evened the playing field a bit.

When he spotted the pair at last, his heart seemed to climb into his throat. Still the consummate professional, she was wearing a bright red suit accessorized with a twist of chunky, expensive gold at the neckline. Her hair had been pulled back into what had probably started as a neat style. Now stray wisps had tugged free to create wayward curls.

And, though she looked as if she were dressed to step into a courtroom or the pages of a career woman's magazine, the expression on her face as she listened to Davey was what stunned him. She looked genuinely entranced, that generous mouth of hers curved into a smile, her eyes bright with amusement. Whatever his son was saying obviously delighted her.

When she laughed, the pure, musical sound carried to him, and he regretted more than he could say that he hadn't been in on the joke.

He walked slowly toward them, feeling like an outsider. When she glanced up and saw him, the sparks in her eyes didn't die as he'd anticipated. Instead, her smile broadened to include him, a touch of sunshine that warmed him.

Basking in that smile could be dangerous, he thought for a fleeting instant, and then he simply responded to its sheer magic. Cares slid away and for this moment, his family was whole again, untouched by sorrow, united by love and laughter. He was a man used to living in a world that made fantasy seem like reality. He realized with a start that he wanted this particular illusion to last more than he'd wanted anything in a very long time.

"Hey, Dad, did you know that Kate has a house at the beach?" Davey said excitedly. "She said we could use it sometime. Wouldn't that be great?"

David met her gaze and wondered at the generosity. "It would be great," he agreed. "But I'm sure Ms. Newton likes to get away herself on the weekends."

"We could all go together," Davey said eagerly. He glanced at Kate. "Is there enough room?"

"Sure," she said.

Despite the quick response, David caught the sudden uneasiness in her eyes. He doubted if her impulsive offer had taken into account this possible turn of events. Lazy days, sun-kissed sand, sparkling blue Pacific... and the two of them. It was the most seductive arrangement he could imagine. If dinner had made her nervous, he could just imagine her reaction to this proposal.

He couldn't resist giving her a long, level, considering look that left no doubts about the provocative direction in which his imagination had roamed. The color that crept into her cheeks almost matched her suit.

"I'm starved," she said in a breathless rush. "Shall we go inside? I made the reservation for seven."

Over their meal, it was Davey's chatter that filled the silences. David hadn't felt quite so tongue-tied in years. As for Kate, he had the feeling she had deliberately withdrawn in an effort to encourage conversation between father and son. Either that or she was still in shock over his deliberately flirtatious glance earlier. He was a little shaken by it himself.

"Shouldn't we discuss this proposal you two have made?" he asked finally, drawing the paper from his pocket.

Davey glanced nervously toward Kate. "It was just some ideas," he mumbled.

"Breakfast every morning?" David read. "I thought you liked sleeping in, during the summer."

"Yeah, I guess."

"Why don't we agree that we'll have breakfast together on the weekends, at least until school starts? Then we'll aim for every day."

Davey's expression brightened. "You promise?"

"I'll put it in writing," David agreed with a pointed look at Kate. "Now, about bedtime. I think I can arrange my schedule to be home on time most nights. I'll even try to make it for dinner.''

"Every night?" Kate inquired.

David shook his head. "I have to be realistic. Let's aim for two nights, plus weekends." He regarded her evenly. "Do you plan to be around to check up on my follow-through?"

"It's my client you have to satisfy, not me. If he tells me you're living up to the agreement, that will be good enough for me."

"Too bad," he found himself taunting. "I'd try harder if I knew I'd find you all curled up in my chair the way I did last night."

She scowled at him. "Keep reading. There are more requests."

"Ah, yes, the once-a-month outings." He glanced at Kate and couldn't resist another attempt to provoke that embarrassed tint in her cheeks. "Why not start with that visit to the beach?"

"Yeah!" David chimed in enthusiastically.

Kate looked stunned.

David regarded her innocently. "Are you busy this weekend?"

She swallowed hard. "This weekend..." Her words faltered. Then her chin came up and she shot him a determined smile. "This weekend would be fine."

No sooner had she agreed than David wondered if he'd lost his mind. Not three hours earlier he'd sworn to stay as far away from this woman as he possibly could. Now he'd committed himself to spending an entire weekend in her company. It was only minimal consolation that she didn't look any more thrilled about the prospect than he did. Only Davey looked ecstatic.

Suddenly David wanted to get out of the dark restaurant and into the twilight and fresh air. "Why don't we have ice cream for dessert?" he suggested. "We can get cones outside."

"All right!" Davey said. "Can I go now?"

"Sure. Just don't go anywhere else. Get the cone and sit at one of the tables right there. We'll be out as soon as I've paid the bill."

Davey grabbed the money his father held out, then took off.

"I could go with him," Kate offered, glancing a little desperately in the direction Davey had gone.

"No. Actually, I wanted a minute alone with you."

Troubled eyes met his. "Oh?"

"I wanted to apologize. I backed you into a corner."

"Yes," she said bluntly. "You did." She shook her head. "No. I made the suggestion in the first place. I guess I just thought you and Davey would go there alone."

"We could still do that," he offered reluctantly. "We would have more fun, though, if you were there. At least, I know I would."

She studied him intently. Obviously she had caught something in his voice, something he hadn't intended to convey with the mildly provocative comment.

"You say that almost as if you're afraid to be alone with your son," she said finally. "It's not the first time

I've noticed that. Were you always so uncomfortable around Davey?''

Startled by her insight, David sighed. "No," he admitted. "We used to do a lot of stuff together. But ever since Alicia died, I don't know what to say to him."

"He's a person. Talk to him about school. Talk about the weather."

"That would be faking it. We both know the one thing we should be talking about is his mother."

"Then for God's sake, talk about his mother," she said with obvious impatience. "Do you know how desperately he needs to share his heartache with you?"

Raw anguish ripped through him as he struggled with what should have been a simple request. He deliberately took his time counting out money to pay the bill. Then he cast one quick look into Kate's eyes and caught the lack of comprehension.

"I can't," he said simply and walked away, leaving her staring after him.

Chapter Five

Kate wanted to sit right where she was until hell froze over. She wanted to do almost anything, in fact, except walk out of the restaurant and join Davey and his father. She wasn't sure she could bear seeing that expression of anguish on David's face.

Worse, to her amazement and regret, she realized that for a few brief moments she had allowed herself to indulge in the fantasy that this was her personal life, not her job. Unlike all those business dinners she had four and five nights a week, sitting here with David and his son tonight had given her a small hint of what it might be like to be part of a normal, ordinary family.

Then Alicia's name had entered the conversation

and reality had intruded with the force of a hurri-
cane-strength wind.

That's what happens when you lose your objectivity, she chided herself. She had set herself up like a
tenpin in a tournament of bowling champions. There
was no way not to get knocked down. The irony, of
course, was that it had been a fantasy which might
never have crossed her mind a week ago, before a desperate, lonely boy had walked into her office.

Forcing herself to put her own bruised feelings
aside, she left the restaurant and went in search of her
client ... and his father. She found them sitting at a
table in front of the ice-cream counter. The last rays of
sunlight filtered through an evening haze. A breeze
had kicked up, chasing away the last of the day's dry
heat. Davey's expression was glum. His father's, if
anything, was even more morose, an echo of her own
feelings.

It had certainly turned into a swell evening, Kate
thought miserably. She forced a smile. "Where's my
ice cream?" she demanded, feigning a fierce scowl.
She glanced at David. "You don't have any, either.
Did Davey eat all they had?"

The weak joke didn't even earn a halfhearted smile.

"I was waiting for you," David said. The response
was politely innocuous, but there was a questioning
look in his eyes as if he wasn't sure what to make of
her teasing or the strained note behind it. "Name your
flavor."

"Heath bar," she said at once. "How about you?
I'll get it." She wanted another minute to gather the

composure that seemed to slip a notch every time she looked into David Winthrop's eyes. To her relief, he didn't argue with her.

"Cherry Garcia."

"Cone or dish?"

"Cone," he said.

When she came back to the table with the two ice-cream cones, Davey and his father were engaged in a tense discussion that broke off the minute she arrived. She handed David his cone and sat down, concentrating on the rapidly melting ice cream. She tried to catch all the drips before they slid down the cone toward her already sticky fingers. It was hopeless. She glanced over and saw that David was having the same problem. As he caught a drip with the tip of his tongue, he gazed into her eyes and smiled. Kate's heart thumped unsteadily at the innocently provocative gesture. She had to force herself to look away.

It was several minutes before she realized that Davey hadn't said a word since she'd joined them. She glanced at him. His arms were folded across his middle and, if anything, his expression had turned mutinous.

"What's the deal, kiddo?" Kate inquired, wondering what on earth they'd fought about.

He glanced at his father with a belligerent look, then said, "Dad says it was rude that we invited ourselves to your house. He doesn't think we should go."

Relief and dismay shot through Kate in equal measure. Then she caught the unhappiness in Davey's eyes and forced herself to put her own conflicting emotions aside and focus on his feelings. He'd already suffered more than enough disappointments in his young life. No matter how trapped she'd felt earlier, she wouldn't add one more by reneging on the invitation. She looked directly at David.

"I want you to come," she said.

His expression told her nothing, but he nodded finally as if he, too, was aware that his son needed the promise of this weekend to be kept. "If you insist," he responded, his tone as cool and unemotional as her own.

Kate stood up, anxious to escape the escalating tension that seemed to be choking off her ability to breathe. "I really need to get some work done tonight, if you two will excuse me." She met David's gaze. "I'll call you about this weekend."

When she looked back as she turned the corner, father and son were sitting silently exactly where she'd left them. It was becoming increasingly obvious that she could throw the two of them together all she wanted, but getting them to have a real relationship again just might be beyond her control. There weren't many things in her life about which that could be said. She discovered she didn't like it.

The phone was ringing when Kate walked into her apartment. She debated letting the service pick it up, then decided that would only delay the inevitable. Whoever it was, she would wind up having to call them back.

She grabbed for the phone on its third ring. "Yes, hello."

"Kate, it's Ellen," her sister said unnecessarily. "Are you okay? You sound out of breath."

"I just ran in the door," she said, wishing she had let the phone go on ringing after all.

Ever since she had learned the whole story behind Ellen's conception, Kate had felt awkward around her older sister. Half-sister, she corrected. Now their mother was married to the love of her life, Ellen's natural father, Brandon Halloran. Ellen, after her initial shock and anger over years of lies and deception, seemed to have adjusted beautifully to having a new father. In fact, she was all caught up in the drama and romance of their mother's separation from Brandon and his intensive search to find her again. Despite everyone's best efforts, however, Kate couldn't help feeling like a resentful outsider.

"I tried to get you earlier," Ellen said. "I wanted to ask you to dinner."

"Sorry," she said, thinking of the unanswered messages she'd allowed to accumulate because she couldn't think of what to say to Ellen these days. "I couldn't have come anyway. I had dinner with a client."

"You work too hard."

"What else is new?" Kate stated with a shrug, kicking off her shoes and wiggling her toes in the cool plush carpet. There was something pleasantly sensuous about the act. "That's the kind of business I'm in."

"Ever think about getting out?" Ellen asked. "Getting married? Settling down?"

"No," Kate said, though less firmly than she might have a few weeks or even a few days ago.

"You should. Dealing with all those unhappy people all the time can't be much fun. Anyway, how about tomorrow? Just you and me and Penny," she suggested, referring to Kate's precocious niece, who displayed every indication of turning into a damn fine trial lawyer herself, if her nosy interrogations into everyone else's personal lives were any clue. Kate didn't think she was up to that sort of teasing scrutiny.

"I really can't, Ellen. This week is jammed up."

"This weekend, then," her sister suggested. The casual persistence was underscored by a hint of genuine dismay over Kate's constant excuses. It was evident Ellen saw right through them.

"I'm having a client out to the beach," Kate said, phrasing it in the most innocuous way she could think of. "Maybe next week." To shift her sister's attention to something else, she asked, "What have you heard from Mother?"

There was a hesitation, as if Ellen wanted to call her on making yet another excuse, but then she sighed. "She phoned this morning from Rome. Can you believe it? Our mother is turning into a world traveler at this stage in her life. Isn't it great?"

"Great," Kate echoed, suddenly feeling even more depressed. "Look, I've got to run. I have a ton of paperwork to get through tonight. I'll be up until all hours.''

Ellen didn't respond for a full minute. If it had been anyone else, Kate might have hung up. Instead, she waited.

"Kate, we're going to have to talk about it one of these days," Ellen said finally.

"I don't know what you mean," Kate said stiffly. "Good night, sis."

She hung up hurriedly and then faced the fact that in one way at least she and David were very much alike. Neither of them seemed able to face the painful truths in their lives.

At five o'clock on Thursday Kate sat at her desk, staring at her calendar and trying to work up the courage to place the call to David Winthrop that would finalize their weekend plans. Zelda found her with her hand in midair over the phone.

"Don't you dare get on that phone again," her secretary ordered. "We have things to discuss, and I've been trying to catch up with you all day."

Grateful for the reprieve, Kate sat back. "What's up?"

"The Winthrop case. What's happening?"

It was the last thing Kate wanted to discuss, especially with Zelda. "Things are moving along," she said evasively. "The father has agreed to spend more time with Davey."

"*The father,*" Zelda mimicked. "Last I heard, the man had a name."

"David," Kate said dutifully.

"Do you have another meeting scheduled with the two of them?"

"Actually, that's what I was calling to arrange when you came in."

"Don't let me stop you, then," Zelda said, though she didn't budge from right where she could listen to every last word of Kate's end of the conversation. Apparently her finely honed instincts for gossip were operating in overdrive.

"Haven't you ever heard of privacy?" Kate grumbled.

"I've had four roommates. What do you think?"

Kate rolled her eyes.

Zelda observed her lack of action and quickly put her own particular spin on it. "If this call were going to, let's say, Jennifer Barron, would you have this same problem about me being in the room?" she inquired, referring to another of Kate's clients.

"You've made your point," Kate retorted. "Now leave."

"Not until you explain why you want to talk to David Winthrop in private."

"If I felt like explaining, then I wouldn't need the privacy, would I?"

Zelda grinned. "Fascinating." She moved reluctantly toward the door. "How about if I leave this open just a crack? I probably couldn't pick up every word."

"I don't want you picking up any words," Kate retorted.

"It gets better and better. You know I could call and schedule the appointment for you. It would save you the trouble."

"Zelda, there are at least a dozen executive secretaries in this building alone who could replace you in less time than it's taking you to leave this room," Kate warned, fully aware that they both knew she was grossly exaggerating. No one could replace Zelda. The threat lost a little of its oomph because of it, but Zelda dutifully closed the door. All the way.

Kate called David's office. She immediately recognized the voice of the woman who answered. It was the same one she'd met the first night she'd charged in there.

"Hi, it's Kate Newton. Is Mr. Winthrop available?"

"Why, Ms. Newton, hello," the assistant said in a tone that rivaled Zelda's for openly friendly curiosity. "I'm Dorothy Paul, his assistant. He's in the back using the chain saw. He'll never hear me buzz. I'll have to get him. Do you mind waiting or shall I have him call you back?"

"I'll wait," she said, unable to hide a grin at the image the woman had raised by mentioning the chain saw. It was fortunate Kate knew what David did for a living. The reference might be very disconcerting for anyone who didn't.

She heard an intake of breath and realized that David's assistant was still on the line.

"Before I get David, I hope you won't mind me butting in, but I wanted you to know that I think you're good for him." She laughed. "He'll kill me for telling you that."

Kate chuckled despite herself. "Actually, I think you couldn't be more wrong. He thinks I'm a nuisance."

"Exactly," Dorothy said. "No one else has braved that don't-bother-me front he puts on."

"Except you," Kate guessed.

"I am fifty years old, fifteen pounds overweight and happily married. He has never looked at me the way he looks at you."

"With disdain," Kate retorted. "I should hope not."

"No. With fascination," she insisted. "Don't give up on him."

Kate felt it important that she clear up Dorothy Paul's misconception about her relationship with David. "I don't think you understand. Our dealings are strictly professional."

The woman chuckled. "Yes. That's what he says, too," she said, her skepticism evident. "I'll get him now."

While she waited, Kate told herself that she had successfully squelched any personal fascination with David Winthrop. There was no reason at all to view the coming weekend as anything more than three acquaintances relaxing and getting to know each other better. It was not the first time she had invited clients or colleagues to visit the beach house. That was one of the reasons she'd bought it in the first place, in fact.

David's grumbled hello sent goose bumps scurrying over her flesh. The effect immediately put an end to any illusions she might have been manufacturing about him being any other business associate.

"I promised to call about the weekend," she said, sounding as if she were the one who'd had to dash for the phone.

"Right," he said matter-of-factly. "This really isn't necessary, you know."

"I think it is."

"Okay, then. What works for you?"

"Can you get out there about seven or seven-thirty tomorrow night? I'll pick up some steaks and we can barbecue on the deck."

"We'll be there. Don't worry about wine or beer. I'll bring that. Anything else you'd like me to bring?"

"No. I keep it pretty well stocked. There are plenty of games and things for Davey, too. There's even a basketball hoop over the garage, if you want to play."

"You entertain a lot of kids?"

"My sister's girls."

"They play basketball?"

"No," she retorted. "I do."

He chuckled. "Now there's a challenge if ever I've heard one."

"Take me on, if you dare," she shot back, then hung up while their shared laughter was still ringing in her ears. Suddenly, despite the loud clang of warning bells, she could hardly wait for the weekend to arrive.

She called Zelda back into her office. "Can you clear my calendar for tomorrow?"

"Any particular time?"

"All day."

Zelda's mouth dropped open in astonishment. "The whole day? Are you sick?"

"No. I just have some things I need to do. I thought I'd take a long weekend at the beach to catch up."

As if she'd already linked Kate's request with that call to David Winthrop and sniffed romance as a result, Zelda immediately grabbed the appointment book and scanned the entries. "You don't have anything in court. No depositions. It looks to me as if I can reschedule your appointments."

"Do it," Kate said, ignoring the speculative gleam in her secretary's eyes. Going to Malibu first thing in the morning would give her a chance to make sure the house was in order.

It would also give her time for a long run on the beach, maybe a swim. Hopefully a little exercise would put an end to all these ridiculous fantasies before the object of those fantasies turned up.

Chapter Six

Running didn't help. Neither did swimming. By seven o'clock on Friday night, Kate was as jittery as a teenager on her first date. Why, she wondered, had an intelligent, cynical woman become attracted for the first time in years to the one man least likely to offer himself heart and soul to a relationship? A man whose behavior toward his son represented the epitome of irresponsibility, if not outright neglect?

She tried telling herself it wasn't attraction so much as determination to help Davey in any way she could. If that meant she had to insinuate herself into his father's life to assure that David and his son forged a new bond, then that's what she would do. She almost believed the explanation. It sounded noble, professional, compassionate. And, in fact, that much really was true. However, despite all the claims she'd made to Dorothy Paul, it wasn't the whole truth by any means.

It was the lost, faraway look in his eyes, she decided after careful analysis. That sorrow hinted at a depth of emotion that some part of her desperately wanted to experience, at the very least wanted to comprehend. And maybe, in some small measure, it was his unavailability. Perhaps she was merely responding to the challenge of conquering that had appealed to men and women from the beginning of time.

The sun was sinking in a rare clear sky when she heard a car pull into the space next to hers along the narrow beachfront road that forked off Pacific Coast Highway. Barefoot and wearing loose white pants and an oversize rose-colored sweater, she walked along the side of the house to the back and opened the gate. She was just in time to see Davey bound around the trendy four-wheel-drive wagon parked next to her expensive low-slung sports car. The ultimate Hollywood, two-car family, she thought wryly, one practical vehicle, the other fast and sexy.

"This place is the best," Davey announced, his eyes sparkling as he bounced up and down on his sneakers as if he couldn't quite wait for the starting gun in a race.

She grinned at his exuberance. "You haven't even seen it yet."

"But I can tell already. Dad says you have a basketball hoop. Can I play? You and me against him, okay? He said you had games, too. What kind? Maybe we could play Monopoly after dinner.''

Kate grinned at his nonstop plans. ''If you think I'm playing Monopoly with you again, you're crazy, kiddo. You're obviously destined to be some sort of real estate tycoon. My ego can't take that kind of bashing.''

Just then David emerged from the car. He was wearing the same style of snug jeans he always wore, topped by a polo shirt in a soft jade green. Somehow, though, he already looked more relaxed, as if he had caught some small measure of his son's excitement.

He surveyed her from head to toe, a surprisingly approving glint in his eyes. That glint told Kate she'd made a mistake when she'd dressed, after all. She'd thought the loose-fitting clothes would be less provocative.

''I suspect your ego could withstand all sorts of assaults,'' he taunted.

The surprisingly lighthearted comment seemed to set the tone for the day. Kate's mood shifted from anxious to something closer to anticipation.

''Surely losing a game to a mere boy wouldn't be enough to shatter your self-confidence,'' he added.

''Has your son ever bankrupted you twenty minutes into a game of Monopoly?'' she inquired dryly.

''Afraid not. I taught him everything he knows.''

Kate scowled as both males grinned unrepentantly. ''How about cards? I'm very good at rummy.''

"We have a whole long weekend to discover all the things at which you excel," David retorted, his speculative gaze leveled on her.

Whatever distance he'd managed to put between them the other night went up in flames. The innuendo sent a shiver straight down her spine. Kate wasn't sure which startled her more, the fact that he'd said it or her own immediate and unmistakably sensual response.

He glanced at her car, and his eyes lit up with an excitement that almost matched Davey's for the house. "Obviously one thing at which you excel is your taste in cars. This is a beauty."

He touched the finish with a certain reverence. Kate found herself envying the sleek metal bumper. He leaned down and peered inside.

"What's it do?"

Kate assumed he was referring to speed. "On our freeways?" she said dryly.

"Yeah. You have a point." With obvious reluctance he turned away from the car. "Davey, have you got all your things?" he asked.

For the next few minutes, they were busy unloading the car and settling the two guests into their rooms.

"If you're hungry, I have dinner set to go," Kate said as the long, empty evening stretched ahead of them. She wanted to cram those hours with activity so that lingering glances could be kept to a minimum, so that these little thrills of pleasure that shot through her at having the two of them there wouldn't escalate into something more. There had to be some way to keep the weekend from ending with her yearning for things that could never be.

"Can we wait?" Davey begged. "I want to see the ocean. Please."

David shook his head. "You'd think you'd never seen the Pacific before."

"It's been a long time, Dad. A really long time. It was before..." His voice trailed off and his father's face went still.

Kate leapt into the sudden silence. "I think a walk on the beach would be the perfect way to work up an appetite. Let's go before it gets too dark."

With Davey running on ahead of them, Kate fell into step beside David. He'd shoved his hands into the pockets of his jeans. The sea gulls circled lazily overhead and a fine mist blew into their faces as they strolled by outrageously expensive homes crammed on the edge of a cliff. Most clung to just enough land to qualify as a homesite, with massive pilings shoring up the bulk of the house. Kate shivered as she considered what was bound to happen one of these days when a violent storm struck.

"Cold?" he asked, misjudging the cause of her trembling.

"No. I was just thinking of what a bad storm would do to this property. Actually, I like chilly nights like this," she confessed. "It's so miserably hot in the city this time of year that I find this thoroughly refreshing. Some nights there's enough briskness in the air to justify a fire. That's always seemed really decadent to me somehow."

He studied her intently. "You love it out here, don't you?"

She nodded. "You sound as if that surprises you."

He shrugged. "I would have thought the rhythm of the city suited you more."

She laughed. "I love that, too. I guess I'm just greedy. I want it all. I want days that are so crowded with work I can't even find time to breathe, and then I want leisurely, do-nothing days that require nothing more than plunking into a chaise longue with a good book and a view of the ocean."

"Be honest," he said. "When was the last time you really had a relaxing, do-nothing day?"

Kate searched her memory. She couldn't think of one, at least not recently.

"Stumped you, didn't I?" David said.

His laughter caught on the wind. He seemed delighted by the discovery that she apparently never followed the exact advice she was giving him.

"I don't have a son around who needs my attention," Kate reminded him.

"Is that the only reason for time off? What about just restoring your own energy, pampering yourself?"

"No time," she admitted.

"Then perhaps this weekend will turn out to be a lesson for both of us," he said, his expression softening. "Now tell me what else you would do, if you really took a vacation. Mountain climbing? That seems like the sort of challenge that would appeal to you."

"Afraid not. I prefer my dangers to come in the form of unexpected evidence. What about you? Mountains? Seaside?"

"No real preference. I live in a world of make-believe most of the time. Always have. I guess what always kept me grounded in reality in any way at all was family. It didn't seem to matter where we were."

"Were you an only child?" she asked, studying him with new perspective.

He regarded her with obvious amazement. "Now, how would you guess a thing like that?"

"It's always seemed to me that an only child might spend a lot of time making up fantasy worlds. Am I right?"

"You're right. And the make-believe worlds kept me from being lonely. Maybe that's why I retreated into one job right after the other once Alicia died. Those worlds are safe, protected. And they're mine to control. I can make them be anything I want them to be."

Control, she thought. There it was again. It seemed to be something they were both intent on having in their lives. "But you have a son, and he didn't get to go along," she reminded him.

"No," he said regretfully. "I suppose he didn't."

She thought she heard real sincerity in his voice and saw an opportunity to forge yet another connection between him and his son. "Could I make a suggestion?"

He grinned at her hesitance. "Nothing's stopped you before."

"If it's still too painful for you to live in the real world full-time, couldn't you take Davey into your world occasionally? I'm sure he would be fascinated to see the sets you create coming to life on a sound-stage. He'd probably be the envy of all his friends for getting a sneak peek at movies that are already being talked about."

To her relief he exhibited absolutely no resistance to the idea. In fact, he pounced on it.

"Would you come along?" he asked lightly. "Would you be interested in seeing my worlds?"

"If you and Davey wanted me to."

He shook his head. "That's not what I asked. I asked if *you* wanted to come along."

"Yes," she admitted, leaving it at that. She didn't want him to see how very curious she was becoming about everything that made him tick. She pushed for a firm commitment, knowing just from what she'd observed of him so far that once he'd made one, he wouldn't back down. "Next week?"

"I'll set it up." His gaze was suddenly warm and approving. "I'm beginning to think it's entirely possible that I had you pegged all wrong," he said slowly, stopping and turning to face her. He reached out to brush the windblown wisps of hair from her face.

Kate's breath snagged in her throat. "Meaning?"

"I thought Davey was just another high-profile case for you, but you honestly care about his feelings, don't you?"

As he spoke, his thumb almost absently caressed her lower lip. Even if she'd been able to form a coherent thought, she wouldn't have risked speaking and breaking that gentle contact. She nodded finally.

"Why?" he asked, lowering his hand to his side with obvious reluctance. He looked almost as shaken as she felt.

Kate shrugged, unable to form a clear response. "I don't really know," she said finally. "He touched me in a way no client has before. I suppose all the people I usually represent are old enough to bear some responsibility for whatever plight they find themselves in. At least they chose their spouse. Davey didn't get to pick his parents. I figure he got a raw deal losing one at such a young age. I couldn't bear to see him losing the other one, especially when it didn't have to be that way."

David's gaze lingered and then he nodded. "Point taken."

She regarded him intently. "I hope so, David. I really hope so, for Davey's sake and for yours. It seems to me you have a pretty terrific kid."

"Yeah," he said, his gaze fixed on the boy who was playing tag with the waves up ahead. "Yeah, I do."

David wasn't sure what name to put on the feeling that was stealing through him. Peace? Contentment? Maybe even a smidgen of anticipation?

Davey had trounced all over both him and Kate playing Monopoly. David blamed it on being distracted. He hadn't been able to keep his eyes off Kate all evening. Now, with an exhausted Davey tucked in, they were alone. Each of them had retreated into work, after a flurry of nervous apologies.

He glanced over at her again. Her cheeks were pink, flushed first by their brisk walk on the beach, then by the color that rose every time she sensed him staring at her. Her hair was carelessly tousled in a way she would never have allowed it to be in the city. Whatever makeup she'd worn earlier had faded, until only her natural beauty showed through. Her bare feet, the toenails painted a soft, feminine shade of rose, were tucked under her. Her lips, curved down in a thoughtful frown as she concentrated on some legal paperwork, suddenly seemed exceptionally kissable. The script he'd been sent for an upcoming feature film couldn't begin to compete for his attention.

He fought against an onslaught of guilt. Dorothy's words came back to him, a reminder that Alicia would never begrudge him a future filled with whatever happiness he could seize for himself and his son. Still, a lawyer? Especially one with a go-for-the-jugular reputation?

And yet all night he had been forced to reassess Kate Newton. She'd been constantly surprising him, both with her compassion for Davey and with her insights. Now, as she sat curled up in a chair, she presented yet another image. Quiet, serene and approachable. All evidence of the prickly, consummately professional attorney had been softened, tempered in this comfortable environment.

Even the house had surprised him. He'd expected something huge and new, a showcase, something so modern and sterile that he would have worried about leaving fingerprints on all the glass and chrome.

Instead, the house was small compared to the newer monstrosities jammed on either side. The decor was an attractive blend of wicker and overstuffed cushions covered in a sturdy, simple Haitian cotton. Every piece of furniture invited relaxation. Colorful pillows added to the cozy allure. To a man sensitive to the uses of color and design, the house offered up the perfect casual, homey beachfront ambience. He wondered if her apartment in the city was the same or offered a contrast to suit her professional persona.

Suddenly he realized that she was regarding him intently.

"I thought you were working," she chided. "Instead, you seem lost in thought."

"That is how I work," he reminded her with a grin, not entirely willing to confess that he hadn't thought of work in quite some time now.

She shook her head. "Of course. I forgot. Is the script any good?"

Now she had him. "I'm not far enough into it to tell yet," he hedged.

"How will you know if it's something you want to work on?"

"If the images start to come."

"And they haven't yet?"

"Not for the movie," he said, surprised a little himself as the faintly provocative words slipped out.

"So, you weren't working," she accused, her eyes dancing with merriment, the golden sparks lighting them from within. "What were you thinking about?"

"Are you sure you want to know?"

"I wouldn't have asked if I didn't."

"You."

"Oh," she said, her voice suddenly whispery soft, even though she didn't look nearly as startled as he'd expected her to.

"No more questions?" he prodded.

"Sure," she said, lifting a bold gaze to clash with his. "Elaborate."

"I was wondering if your apartment in the city suited you as well as this place does."

A startled expression crossed her face. "I never really thought about it."

"Let me guess, then. Very elegant. Very tasteful. Very expensive. Maybe a few Oriental touches, along with some European antiques. The finest wood."

She laughed. "Have you been peeping in windows?"

"Nope. I just know where all the top decorators hang out."

"What makes you think I didn't choose that for myself?"

"You wouldn't waste the time." Her expression told him he was right.

"And this place?" she challenged.

"This, I think, you did yourself. I think you picked things because they appealed to your sense of color and touch or maybe just for fun," he said, glancing at a colorful child's pinwheel that had been used instead of flowers in a tall vase in one corner.

"A gift from my youngest niece," she admitted. "It was accompanied by an automatic bubble gun. She thinks I'm too stuffy." She hesitated, then added, "I get the impression that you think that, too."

"Does it matter to you what I think?" he asked, allowing his gaze to linger warmly until he sensed the color rising in her cheeks again. It felt good to engage in this sort of flirtatious bantering with a woman again, especially with one who seemed almost as new to it as he was.

There was an instant's panic in her eyes before that stubborn chin of hers tilted up a notch. "Yes. I think perhaps it does," she admitted, leaving him almost speechless at the rare hint of vulnerability she'd displayed.

Such candor deserved an honest response. David considered his answer carefully. "My impression of you is changing by the minute," he said slowly. "I'm beginning to think you are a rather remarkable woman, Kate Newton."

She looked startled and pleased. "Really?"

"Definitely remarkable," he said as he rose to his feet and walked across the room. He held out his hands, and after an instant's hesitation she placed hers in them. He drew her up. "I don't know what the hell is happening here, but I don't think I can wait one more minute to kiss you."

Her eyes widened, but she didn't pull away, seemingly every bit as mesmerized as he was. Stunned by the force of his need after months and months of abstinence, he slanted his mouth over hers.

Her lips were every bit as soft and yielding as he'd imagined. The texture was like satin, warmed and rumpled by a night of steamy sex. The taste? Sweet, with an intoxicating hint of the wine they'd had with dinner. It had been so long since he'd kissed anyone other than his wife that the sensations felt totally new, more vivid and soul-stoppingly pleasurable than anything he remembered.

He drew back and looked into her eyes, saw the faint stirring of passion and sensuality, that startled look of amazement that told him she was as taken aback as he by whatever was happening between them. Unwilling to let those feelings fade when they'd only just discovered them, he scooped up handfuls of that luxurious, silky black hair as he framed her face and settled his lips over hers once more.

There would be time enough tomorrow and the day after that and on into the weeks ahead for all the regrets that were bound to follow.

Chapter Seven

Thank God for Davey, Kate thought as she sat across the breakfast table from David in embarrassed silence. For a woman not easily rattled, those kisses the night before had shaken her in ways she'd never imagined possible. She'd been awake half the night thinking about them. At least Davey's presence prevented a morning-after analysis of the mistake in judgment they'd made by allowing the intimacy of those kisses.

Why the devil hadn't she thought to set ground rules for herself, as well as him? Possibly because it had never occurred to her that David viewed her as anything other than a prospective adversary in a battle over his son's future. She wondered for one fleeting instant if those kisses had been part of some low-down, scheming tactics to throw her off guard. She dismissed the idea almost as soon as it had formed. Nothing she'd seen thus far had suggested that David was anything but a man of real character, albeit one who'd lost sight of his priorities for a brief time.

None of that explained her own behavior. She had wanted him to kiss her, had practically set the stage and invited him to, with her taunting remarks. She never did things like that. Never!

Davey looked from Kate, who was sweeping scrambled eggs from one side of her plate to the other without lifting so much as a forkful to her mouth, to his father, who was crumbling a piece of toast in a similarly distracted manner.

"You guys are acting weird," Davey declared.

He was right on target. Kate glanced up, found her gaze clashing with David's, and forced her attention to his son. "That's because we're both in a state of shock after the way you stole every piece of property we'd accumulated last night," she improvised, rather well she thought.

"Stole it!" he exclaimed indignantly. "I bought it. Can I help it if you managed to go bankrupt trying to stay out of jail and paying off rental charges every time you landed on my property?"

"Your overdeveloped property," Kate retorted. She shot David a conspiratorial glance. "Next time, I say we demand zoning laws."

"Rigid zoning laws," David agreed. "And I personally intend to check those dice today to see if you tampered with them. Nobody should have the run of luck you had.''

Davey's eyes danced with impish laughter. ''You had luck, too, Dad.''

''Oh, really?''

''Yeah, rotten luck.''

His father glowered at him, but with obvious underlying affection. ''Just for that, you're on kitchen duty. Kate and I are going for a walk on the beach. You can come join us when these dishes are done.''

''But I have a dishwasher,'' Kate protested, though Davey didn't seem to regard being relegated to doing the chore as any sort of punishment.

''And Davey can load it,'' David countered. He held out his hand. ''Let's go.''

Kate regarded that outstretched hand as if it represented more danger than a crate of TNT. The last time she'd allowed even such an innocent touch, she'd found herself in an embrace that had taken her breath away. To avert a repeat performance, she grabbed up her dishes and put them on the counter, as close as she could get them to the dishwasher without undermining David's order. She caught the unmistakable gleam of understanding in his eyes as she tried to sashay out the door with no hint of the turmoil she was in.

Outside, with the morning fog still hanging over the ocean, she jammed her hands in her pockets and set off at a brisk pace. She reminded herself sternly that she was a woman who took on powerful men in court all the time without the least trepidation. She reminded herself that David Winthrop was no more powerful, no more threatening than any one of those adversaries.

And then he put his hand on her shoulder and proved her wrong. She felt a jolt of electricity that went clear to her toes. Some dangers obviously had nothing to do with intelligence, courtrooms or adversarial relationships. Some dangers, it seemed, came from within. This man had an innate ability to shake her up with the simplest gesture, the slightest contact. Apparently ignoring those reactions wasn't going to make them go away.

"I'm curious about something," she said eventually.

"Oh?"

"Why did you kiss me last night?"

"Surely a woman as bright as you are can figure that one out," he said, amusement written all over his face. He didn't seem nearly as distressed by what had happened as she did.

"Never assume anything," she shot right back, the comment as much an explanation for her behavior as it was a challenge to him.

"Why does any man kiss a woman?" he asked with a great display of patience. "Because he finds her attractive."

Attraction, she thought. An inexplicable chemistry. She could deal with that. She was attracted to him, too. That didn't mean they had to *do* anything about it.

"Are you suggesting that anytime someone is attracted to another person, they should have free rein to act on those impulses?'' she inquired cautiously just to be sure those ground rules weren't an absolute necessity.

That increasingly familiar tolerant smile crept across his face. "Assuming we're talking consenting adults here, Ms. Attorney, I'd have to say yes," he said.

"Then it could happen again?"

"Oh, I'd say that's almost a certainty." He regarded her intently. "Does that make you nervous?"

Now she was caught in a big-time dilemma. She believed in truth and honesty at all costs. She also believed in preserving some measure of dignity. "Me?" she hedged.

"There's no one else around who looks as jumpy as a Junebug," he observed, giving an exaggerated glance around the deserted beach just to prove his point.

Kate drew in a deep breath. "Okay, let's be honest here."

He looked disgustingly fascinated by the prospect. "By all means," he taunted.

"I can understand your wanting to kiss me." She glanced at him, then away. "You know, the chemistry thing."

"Given your intelligence, I'd be surprised if you couldn't."

"Would you give me a break?" she asked impatiently. In court, the judge would probably charge him with contempt for all the snappy rejoinders. She was stuck with appealing to his sense of fair play. "I'm trying to make a point here."

He held up his hands in a gesture of surrender. "Sorry."

"Okay, then. I can understand one kiss, as an experiment, so to speak."

"Two," he corrected, not even trying to contain that damnable grin. "I distinctly remember two."

Kate did also. Even if she'd been able to bury the fiery memory of one of them, it appeared likely he intended to remind her at each and every opportunity. How had she so badly misread David Winthrop? She'd never guessed that all that sorrow had dimmed the soul of a scoundrel. She'd wanted to draw him out of his self-absorption for his son's sake, not reawaken his slumbering libido for her own.

Of course, who was she to say it had been slumbering? Davey was the one he'd been ignoring. For all she knew, those nights he spent away from home had been spent in the consoling arms of some woman. She scowled at the thought, even as she dismissed it. If she was certain of nothing else, it was that David was every bit as loyal to his wife's memory as he had been to Alicia when she was alive.

"Hey," he said jovially. "One kiss. Two. Who's counting? No need to get testy."

"I am not testy," she said in a tone that contradicted the statement. "Look, all I'm trying to say is that I have a responsibility to my client here. I think there's a real conflict of interest in our..."

Involvement? She wasn't about to even hint at the word. *Kissing?* That sounded absurd, given the way he'd downplayed the activity as little more than a scientific experiment that might need to be repeated indefinitely until some theory or other was proved or disproved.

"Our what?" he prodded.

"I think we should keep our distance," she blurted.

"From an ethical standpoint."

She beamed, delighted that he'd caught on so quickly. "Yes, exactly."

Brown eyes, devoid of so much as a hint of amusement now, studied her intently. "Hogwash!" he said softly, stepping closer and framing her face with his hands.

The warmth of his hands against her skin sent that all-too-familiar, insidious heat flooding through her. She glared at him indignantly and stepped out of reach. "What's that supposed to mean?"

"I thought you intended to be honest."

"I am being honest."

"Hogwash!" he repeated even more adamantly.

The word was really grating on her nerves, especially since it was about as accurate as any she could think of for describing the wimpy speech she'd just given.

"Kate, if you have a problem with me touching you, you'll have to spell it out in a way that doesn't mock *my* intelligence. There is no danger whatsoever of a few kisses influencing the way you handle Davey's case. In fact, if you were being totally honest with me and yourself, you'd admit that the closer you and I become, the more influence you'd have over my relationship with my son."

"But then I'd be open to charges that I'd manipulated you," she said, desperately grabbing at straws.

"Charges by whom?"

"You."

"Not me," he denied. "I don't manipulate so easily, as you'll discover as time goes by." He allowed that to sink in, then added, "Along with a good many other things."

"What?" she said blankly, wondering how she'd lost control not only of this conversation, but quite possibly of her entire life.

"There are a great many things you'll get to know about me," he explained. "Given time."

How much time did the man think this case was going to take? she wondered. She'd hoped to have him and his son on track by the close of the weekend, if only to assure a return of her own equanimity.

"I think we've gotten off track here," she told him firmly. "This weekend isn't about you and me. It's about you and Davey." She turned on her heel. "I'll send him out."

Unfortunately Davey was already out and happily engaged in building a sand fortress with two boys from farther along the beach. That meant David hit the deck approximately fifteen seconds after Kate did. Alone.

"Shall I go drag him away from his new friends so he and I can share some quality time?" he inquired with a hint of mirth sparkling in his eyes.

Since she didn't have a guidebook for this sort of thing, Kate had to go with instinct. As much as she wanted David otherwise occupied, it appeared she was out of luck. Sending him off to intrude on his son's play wouldn't accomplish a thing, except to force them into grudging contact. If Davey was content just knowing his father was nearby, wasn't that good enough?

"There's a ton of books inside. Grab one if you like," she conceded. A man engrossed in a good book would not be ogling her the way he was now.

"I brought one with me," he said. "But I think I'll take a look at what you keep on hand anyway. Bookshelves say a lot about a person."

"Then these will present a very confusing picture," she retorted. "My collection represents the very eclectic tastes of previous guests."

Undaunted, he retorted, "Better yet. You can always tell a person by the company she keeps." He headed inside with a determined glint in his eyes.

He was back in half an hour, not nearly long enough for her to become so absorbed in the mystery that she was reading that she wouldn't notice his arrival. The truth of the matter was that she'd read the same opening paragraph five times without one single word registering. Obviously, whether she liked it or not, David Winthrop was more fascinating.

"What's the verdict?" she asked.

"A woman with this particular circle of friends probably ought to be in analysis," he said dryly. "Do you know anyone who's not in some sort of recovery program or obsessed with bloody true-crime cases?"

"No one I know is in a recovery program. That's why they read so many of those books. They swear it's cheaper than analysis and just as effective. As for the true crime, a lot of my clients are in the entertainment industry. They're always looking for movie material," she explained, then added as an afterthought, "Of course, I can't swear that some of them aren't considering techniques for murdering their spouses at the same time. I try to head that off by getting them very large settlements."

"You obviously perform a great public service, in that case."

She grinned. "I do try." She glanced at the thick, dog-eared book he was carrying. "What are you reading?"

"My beach book," he said without the least hint of apology. "I've been reading this for years. I usually manage about fifty pages per vacation. The rest of the year I don't have time for it."

"Must not be a terribly compelling plot, if you can put it aside for long periods of time," she noted.

"Naval history. That's the great thing about reading history. Once it's recorded, not much changes. I could pick this up ten years from now and it would still be accurate, just farther in the past."

"For a man whose life revolves around whimsy and make-believe that's an awfully staid approach to reading material."

"Balance," he reminded her. "Isn't that exactly what you've been trying to remind me about? We all need a little balance in our lives."

"True," she conceded, and wondered yet again if this wasn't a lesson she needed very much to learn, as well. Perhaps, she thought for the second time that day, perhaps fate had delivered Davey Winthrop into her life not just because of what she could do for him, but for what he and his father might do for her.

Kate was standing under the hot spray of the shower Saturday night, when she heard someone knocking loudly on the bathroom door.

"Kate, phone," David bellowed. "It's long distance from Rome."

Oh, dear Lord, she thought at once. Her mother! And *David* had answered the phone. As she turned off the water and reached for a towel, she could already imagine the mile-long list of questions his presence would arouse.

She pulled on a thick, terry-cloth robe and wrapped her damp hair in a towel. Then, and there was no way around it that she could think of, she opened the bathroom door to face David and her mother, in that order. For the moment he actually seemed less daunting, though a gentleman would have left her bedroom once he'd announced the call. He was lingering in the doorway, arms crossed, an appreciative gleam in his eyes.

"Go away," she murmured as she reached for the phone.

He winked, but he did go away. In fact, she heard the hang-up click of the receiver on the living room

phone before she'd even had a chance to say a breathless hello to her mother.

"Darling, how are you?" Elizabeth Halloran asked.
"And who was that charming man?"

"Charming?" Kate repeated, hearing the distinct
clang of warning bells.

"Absolutely. He asked all about our trip when I told
him I was calling from Rome. He said he'd been here.
He even remembered a little restaurant that he highly
recommended. I think Brandon and I will try it tomorrow. Now, who is he?"

"It's a long story."

Apparently her mother knew her well enough by
now to realize that further probing would be useless.
"Well, I'm just delighted that you're seeing someone.
Brandon will be, too."

"I'm not *seeing* David. He's a client, actually the
father of a client."

"Oh," her mother said with obvious disappointment. "Then I'm sure he's probably too old for you
anyway, dear. That's too bad."

Kate decided against trying to explain, since her
mother seemed willing to forget whatever romantic
fantasy she'd been dreaming up since David had
picked up the phone. She was incredibly grateful for
the reprieve.

"Are you and Brandon having a good time?" she
asked.

Her mother sighed dreamily. "Darling, it's the vacation of a lifetime. I can't tell you how happy he has
made me. Wait until you see all the pictures."

"When are you coming home?" Kate asked, trying not to let a wistful note creep into her voice.

"Not for a while yet, dear. Brandon insists on going to Athens next, then Paris and London. After that, we'll see how exhausted we are."

Kate heard a murmured argument, then Brandon's voice. "Katie, don't you go badgering this woman to come home when I've finally got her to myself after all these years," he teased. "Now what's this I hear about a man being at your place when you're in the shower? What are his intentions?"

She realized the inquiry was vintage Brandon. "I don't think he has any intentions, at least where I'm concerned."

She heard another murmured comment by her mother, then Brandon's deep chuckle and a low retort that had her mother laughing.

"Your mother says he's too old for you anyway," Brandon said. "I just reminded her I'm old, and I wasn't such a bad catch."

"Ah, but you're one of a kind," Kate teased him, finding that despite her reservations, she couldn't help liking the man who was making her mother so happy. "If I could find someone like you, then maybe I'd find marriage more appealing."

"You just sit tight, then, young lady. As soon as I get home, I'll find you somebody who'll treat you the way you deserve to be treated."

Since she didn't have an answer to that except to scream a fervent *no*, Kate muttered a hurried goodbye and prayed that this honeymoon would turn out to be the longest one on record. Knowing Brandon's penchant for meddling, though, he might very well get it into his head to cut it short just to fix up her love life, especially if he sensed it would make her mother happy to see her settled.

She was still sitting on the edge of her bed contemplating the horror of that prospect, when David tapped on the partially opened door and stuck his head in.

"Is that what you're wearing to dinner?" he inquired hopefully.

She glowered at him. "We're casual out here, but we usually do insist on clothes," she retorted. "I'll be ready in a few minutes."

He regarded her quizzically. "Want to tell me why you were looking so sad just now? The call wasn't bad news, was it?"

"Not unless you consider the prospect of a stepfather arranging a marriage for me to be bad news."

David looked incredulous. "You're joking, right?"

"You don't know Brandon. He's getting worried that he'll have a spinster stepdaughter on his hands. If I'm not careful, when they get to Greece he'll provide a herd of sheep and a grove of olive trees as a dowry in return for some suitably old-fashioned Greek husband for me," she said with what was probably only minimal exaggeration. "He'll drag him home along with the more conventional souvenirs."

David gave her a thoughtful look, one that suggested he was considering whether she was worth more or less than that herd of sheep and an olive grove.

"If it comes to that," he said finally, "you tell him to speak to me first. I'll take you without the sheep. I think there's a law against them in Bel Air anyway."

She scowled at him. "I'll keep your generous offer in mind," she retorted dryly.

"On the other hand," he said, "I could use a good dairy cow."

Kate threw her silver hairbrush straight at him. It didn't do a thing to squelch his amusement, but it did get him to close the damned door.

Chapter Eight

Because she did so much weekend entertaining during the summer months, Kate kept a standing reservation for four at Alice's Restaurant on the Malibu Pier for every Saturday night. She called only to cancel or to enlarge the size of her party. She liked the food. She liked the people. And she loved the view, especially in summer when an eight o'clock reservation virtually guaranteed a spectacular sunset display except on the foggiest evenings. On Sundays when she had guests, she took them to Geoffrey's for brunch in the lovely garden setting on a cliff overlooking the sea, but on Saturday night she liked the crowded, lively ambience of Alice's.

Though the staff and many of the regular customers were used to seeing her here, she noticed a few raised eyebrows and speculative glances when she walked in with David and Davey.

Everyone knew that Kate Newton never dated. The painful love affair responsible for her solitude had long since ceased to be a topic of conversation, but it hadn't been forgotten. At the time, almost everyone in certain Hollywood circles had seen the irony in the famed divorce lawyer being caught up in what had nearly become a highly publicized palimony scandal with the creep suing her. Knowing Kate as well as he had, however, had led Ryan Manning to settle out of court and slink off to prey on other unsuspecting women.

As a result of all that thoroughly dissected past history, had she been with David alone, everyone would have guessed him to be an exceptionally handsome colleague or a client and gone back to their dinners.

Davey's presence changed all that. Kate rarely entertained children, other than her nieces. She wasn't regarded as the maternal type, probably because of her cutthroat courtroom reputation. To see her here with father and son, especially this particular father and son, was clearly cause for fascination.

All during dinner people found excuses to drop by the table, angling for introductions, hoping to pinpoint the exact nature of the relationship. Some, she knew, genuinely hoped that she'd found a new, satisfying romance. Others had recognized David and no doubt knew the details of his tragic loss. They clearly wondered if his days of mourning were past.

Kate guessed there would be no fewer than half a dozen calls by Monday morning, at least one of them from a gossip columnist from one of the film industry trade papers. She could barely wait for the meal to end, so she could escape the unspoken speculation.

Davey, however, insisted on dessert. And David wanted coffee. Kate wanted to scream with impatience, but didn't dare. Then she would have to explain exactly why she was suddenly so uncomfortable.

"Kate? Coffee?" David asked as the waiter jotted down the order.

"Please," she said, though she couldn't think of anything she wanted less. But if she had to sit here, she wanted something to do.

"You can have some of my dessert," Davey offered generously. "I probably won't eat it all."

"Right," his father said skeptically. "You never leave me so much as a crumb."

"Because you always say you don't want any and then you start sneaking in with your fork, and before I know it, it's all gone. Then you call me a pig."

Kate relaxed slightly as she chuckled at Davey's indignation. Watching him, she felt a powerful, deep emotion that was entirely new to her. His usually neat hair was windblown. His cheeks and arms were tinted pink from too much sun. He had a scrape on one elbow from falling on the sand during a volleyball game. He had a streak of ketchup on his chin. He was so exhausted he could hardly keep his eyes open, but he looked the happiest she'd ever seen him. He looked like a kid again. The messy, energy-draining kind. The kind she'd always sworn she wanted no part of.

So why did she feel so contented? Why did she look at Davey and feel this gut-wrenching tug of tenderness stealing through her? True, Davey was a pretty extraordinary boy. He was bright, funny and compassionate. He was certainly bold beyond his years. In short, he had a lot of the same traits she'd had at the same age. Her niece, Penny, was similarly precocious. Kate wondered if her own kids would have turned out to be nearly as interesting. Maybe she ought to be grateful she knew kids like Penny and Davey and not even consider testing her own luck with the gene pool.

A rational plan, one she'd embraced long ago, when work had been a demanding, satisfying lover. Tonight, however, Kate wasn't feeling rational. She looked at Davey and his father and wished with all her heart that her life had taken a different track. She sighed at the realization that it was rapidly getting too late to change directions, especially now that she'd been on this lonely course for so long.

"You look as if you're a million miles away," David said, interrupting her disturbing thoughts. "And wherever you are doesn't look like a very happy place."

Kate was startled that he could read her so easily. She must be growing too comfortable with him. Usually she kept her guard up better. It was tiring, but necessary. One of the first lessons she'd learned as a lawyer was never to show her hand in a courtroom.

She'd adopted the same unrevealing mask in her personal life, as well.

Until now.

"Is mind reading one of your talents?" she inquired more irritably than the observation merited.

"It doesn't take much talent when an expression is as easy to interpret as yours was. What were you thinking about?"

"Independence."

"The city or the state of mind?"

"Very funny."

He didn't react visibly to the trace of sarcasm, but his tone was definitely more sober when he asked, "Okay, what exactly were you thinking about independence?"

Kate hesitated to say it aloud. It would sound too much as if she were dissatisfied with her life, and she wasn't. Not really. She was just in a mood, an oddly disturbing mood that she couldn't seem to shake.

"Kate?" he prodded.

She saw that he wasn't going to let the topic drop. "I suppose I was thinking that independence isn't all it's cracked up to be. Sometimes it's very taxing."

He regarded her quizzically, obviously waiting for more.

"Actually, I suppose I was envying you," she confessed, surprising herself with the honesty of the admission. It was the sort of revealing comment she normally would have avoided at all costs.

Astonishment filled his eyes. "Me? Why?"

"You have a career you obviously love. You have your son."

As if he wasn't quite sure how to respond to the rare confession, David glanced at Davey. "A son who is asleep on his feet."

"Am not," Davey said sleepily, his eyelids drooping even as he uttered the denial.

"Maybe we should get the check," David suggested, snagging the last bite of his son's cake. His gaze caught hers. "We can finish this discussion at home."

Home, she thought with raw yearning that hit her like a bolt out of the blue. Until David had used the word, she'd never imbued it with so much meaning. Now she saw that the house she loved so much was just that, a house. It wasn't until just tonight that she'd realized that for the past twenty-four hours it had felt more like a home. Laughter and contentment and warmth had spilled into the rooms.

She sighed heavily. Would she ever feel quite the same way about it, now that they had been there to show her what having a marriage and a family could be like? Or would this odd dissatisfaction and emptiness only be magnified?

"There's nothing to discuss," Kate said, desperately wanting to put an end to the topic before yet another layer of her defenses could be stripped away. As mid-life crises went, it appeared she was plunging headfirst into a real doozy.

* * *

David was up at the crack of dawn on Sunday. He made a pot of Kate's fancy coffee, then took a mug out onto the deck and tried to analyze Kate's retreat the previous night.

She had begun pleading exhaustion the minute they hit the house. Given the shadows in her eyes, he might have believed her if he hadn't seen her light burning and heard her restless pacing long after she'd supposedly gone to bed. He'd guessed then that she desperately wanted to avoid completing the conversation she herself had begun at the restaurant.

She was a real study in contradictions. There had been times this weekend when he'd felt the barriers between them—his and hers—beginning to slip away. He'd enjoyed watching her with Davey, seeing the genuine enjoyment she seemed to get from probing his lively mind. She obviously liked his son. She treated him like a person, rather than a child, and Davey responded to that respect as any kid would.

Davey had wanted Kate to tuck him in before she fled to her own room. And Kate had figured prominently in Davey's prayers, joining his father, his mother and Mrs. Larsen for special mention. Though she had rapidly blinked them away, there had been no mistaking the tears that sprang into Kate's eyes when she'd heard. Right after that she had practically bolted for her room.

Sitting on the deck, sipping his coffee, David admitted that the weekend had been good for him. He felt more relaxed now than he had in months. He and

Kate had fallen into a surprisingly easy rhythm of camaraderie. That sense that he was being disloyal had stolen over him only once or twice, mainly after he had kissed Kate on Friday night and then Saturday when he'd wanted badly to kiss her again just to prove that the first time hadn't been a fluke.

So, he thought, it was just possible that he was going to go on living, no matter how hard he'd tried to bury his emotions along with Alicia. Anything more than that—falling in love, for instance—still seemed beyond him. Perhaps he would never again experience that head-over-heels sensation that had engulfed him the first instant he had laid eyes on Alicia. Maybe things a man had felt at twenty weren't possible at thirty-five.

And yet there was an oddly erratic beat to his heart when Kate Newton walked into a room. It was only a glimmer of what he recalled of those early days with Alicia, but the chemistry was unmistakable just the same. He could leave her today and slam the door on that feeling or he could encourage further contact, explore the sensations and give them time to flourish.

If she'd let him. She, it seemed, was fearful not only of commitment, but of all the stages leading up to it.

He closed his eyes, seeing her as she had been when she'd climbed out of the shower to take that overseas call the night before. He sighed as he recalled how beautiful and sensual she'd looked with her face scrubbed clean, her skin glowing and soft as satin, her slim body given fascinating curves by the added bulk of that terry-cloth robe that shaped itself to her damp flesh. It had taken every ounce of restraint he possessed to resist a quick tug on that robe's loosely tied belt to expose the alluring woman beneath. Even now, just the memory stirred his blood and sent it rushing through him.

While those provocative memories were still taunting him, he thought he imagined the scent of lily of the valley. Then he heard a faint whisper of sound and realized Kate had padded out to join him, her feet bare as usual, her endlessly long legs encased in denim. On top she wore a faded, misshapen UCLA sweatshirt. She settled onto the chaise longue next to his. He opened his eyes and turned toward her.

"Good morning."

She gave him a sleepy smile in return. "You're up early. Couldn't you sleep?"

"Actually, I slept better than I have in ages," he admitted. "The salt air and activity were obviously just what I needed."

She nodded. "I'm glad." She drew her knees up and rested her chin on them. Occasionally she lifted the mug of coffee to her lips, obviously content with the silence and perhaps even with the companionship. Suddenly David wanted to understand what she was feeling, if the weekend had meant anything at all to her.

"Kate?"

"Umm?"

"I find myself in a quandary."

Still she didn't glance at him. "Oh?"

"You could at least act sympathetic," he chided. "I'm not a man who's used to not knowing how to handle something."

"I'm sure," she said, looking not one whit more sympathetic.

"What I'm trying to say here is that I'd like to see you again."

"I'm sure we'll be running into each other all the time," she said, her expression deliberately cool, not giving him an inch, even though he was laying his damned soul bare. To add to the insult, she said, "Given Davey's suit and all."

David lost patience. "Dammit, I'm not discussing having an occasional polite meeting to discuss legal affairs."

"I am."

She had never seemed more distant. He found it infuriating. "Why?"

"Because that's the way it has to be."

"Are we back to the ethics thing again? Or is this because you have no desire to see me on a personal basis? If that's it, Kate, just spit it out and I'll back off."

She turned then, and he could see the conflicting emotions warring in her eyes. She blinked and turned away. "That's not it," she said finally.

"Then for God's sake, explain it to me. It's been a long time since I dated. Maybe all the rules have changed."

"I suspect it's been even longer since I dated, and as far as I know the rules are the same. Given the lack of recent experience for both of us, I think maybe we're grasping at straws here, trying to fill a void in our lives. A couple of kisses don't mean anything, no matter how enjoyable they were.''

"What about the walks? What about the talks? What about playing games with Davey? In my book all of that adds up to two people who are compatible, who have things in common, who are mature enough not to expect bells and whistles.''

She gave him a wry smile. "Bells and whistles may not be mandatory in your book, but I figure that's what gets two people through the rough patches.''

David recalled the passion Alicia had always stirred in him and knew Kate was right. Tempestuous passion and gentle, enduring love went hand in hand in the strongest relationships, forging an unbreakable bond. The memories of the glorious passion he and Alicia had shared were what he had pulled out and held dear when times had gotten tough. Was he any more willing than Kate to settle for less?

He gazed at her intently. "I think perhaps I hear a distant bell ringing,'' he said softly, unable to hide the wistfulness behind the claim. "Shouldn't we try to find it?''

She reached over and touched her fingers to his and all at once the peal of bells seemed more distinct. Her gaze searched his.

"We've both been bruised in very different ways, you more recently than I,'' she said gently. "Let's not rush into something.''

He curved his fingers around hers, liking the way her hand fit in his, liking even more the protectiveness that was stealing through him. "A slow stroll, then," he suggested as their gazes caught and held.

She drew in a deep breath, then slowly exhaled, her shoulders visibly relaxing. When she nodded at last, David felt something burst free deep inside him, and for the first time in a very long time he was filled with hope.

The weekend ended for Kate with the same mix of anticipation and trepidation with which it had begun. She was anxious to see them go. She was torn by the unexpectedly powerful desire to have them stay. Her talk that morning with David had opened up all of the delicious possibilities of the future. It had also stirred all the warning signals of the past. By the time they actually began to load the car she was as limp as a dishrag from dealing with all of the conflicting emotions.

"This was the best weekend of my whole life," Davey declared.

Kate mussed his hair, which he'd brushed back neatly after his shower. "I'm glad you had fun, kiddo."

Suddenly his lower lip quivered. His arms circled her waist and he buried his head against her. "I love you, Kate," he said, his voice muffled.

She felt her throat constrict so tightly that not a single sound could squeeze past. She hugged him tight. "You'll come back," she said when she could finally speak, wishing she dared to lay her own emotions on the line as easily, wishing she even understood what they were. She made the promise of a return as much for herself as she did for Davey. She looked up and saw David watching her, his own eyes suspiciously moist.

"That's right," he said briskly. "We'll be back. And Kate's going to bring you over to see the set for *Future Rock* this week, aren't you, Kate?"

It was the first she'd heard of any specific plan, but she nodded. "Absolutely. Just think, Davey, you and I will get a chance to see something that's the biggest secret in all of Hollywood."

Davey released her then and swiped at the damp traces of tears on his cheeks. His smile wobbled just a little. "You mean it, Dad?"

"Of course I mean it. Kate and I will compare schedules tomorrow and pick a day."

Davey made a fist. "Yes," he said as if he'd just won a victory. He climbed into the wagon and belted himself in. Kate closed the door, then turned to find David waiting for her behind the car.

"Thank you," he said.

"You're welcome."

"I'll call tomorrow."

She nodded.

He stepped closer and cupped the back of her head. Slowly, so slowly that Kate's pulse was thundering with anticipation, he lowered his head and touched his lips to hers. Cool as a breeze, quick as the fleeting brush of a butterfly's wings, the kiss was over almost beforo it began.

And yet she heard the very distinct, if distant, sound of bells.

Chapter Nine

When Kate returned from court at noon on Monday, a full week after her fateful weekend with David and Davey, she found her sister waiting in the conference area of her office. She felt her stomach begin to knot, but she managed what she hoped was a breezy, unconcerned smile as she stepped behind her desk. Even an amateur psychologist would have seen the significance of placing that defensive barrier between her and her sister.

"Ellen, what are you doing here?" she asked, trying unsuccessfully to keep an edge out of her voice.

"We're having lunch," Ellen said in a tone that brooked no argument.

Kate's gaze shot to her, then faltered. "Lunch?" She glanced pointedly at her appointment book. "Oh, dear, I'm sorry if you came all this way hoping to catch me free, but there's an appointment on my calendar with a client."

"Not a client," Ellen declared. "Me. I had Zelda put me down."

There was a stubborn set to her chin that Kate recognized from years of butting heads with her older sister. Though Ellen had been a dreamer and a romantic, when that strong will of hers finally asserted itself, even the indomitable Kate listened.

She glared at Kate. "And don't you dare yell at Zelda for doing it without consulting you. Now put down your briefcase and let's get out of here. I've made reservations at a place that'll probably charge by the minute if we show up late."

Kate gave a sigh of resignation as she accepted the futility of arguing. "You always were the bossiest big sister of anyone we knew," she grumbled.

Ellen shot her an unrepentant grin. "I know. Too bad I let you get the upper hand in recent years. Otherwise, maybe you'd be married by now and I could stop worrying about you."

"Don't you dare start on that," Kate warned as she followed her from the office. She shot a furious look at Zelda on her way to the elevator. For once her secretary seemed amazingly absorbed in her typing.

Ellen had heavily tipped one of the parking valets at the office building to keep her car waiting at the curb. Kate reluctantly climbed in. Now, with no car of her own, she would be totally at Ellen's mercy. She'd have to listen to every last word of whatever lecture or probing interrogation her sister had in mind.

Ellen drove the few blocks into Beverly Hills and whipped into a parking garage as if she made the trip to Rodeo Drive daily, rather than once a year, if that. She had chosen a restaurant just off the famed shopping street. Not until she and Kate were seated did she say another word. Kate was content to let the silence continue as long as possible.

Ellen ordered a glass of wine. Kate ordered bottled mineral water. She wanted a clear head for whatever was to come. When their drinks arrived, they ordered lunch. Ellen took her first sip of the Chardonnay, set down her glass and faced Kate. "Okay, let's hear it."

"Hear what?" Kate evaded. She hadn't arranged this confrontation. She saw no reason to be the first one to put her cards on the table.

Ellen looked disgusted by the evasiveness. "For a woman who can make any bigwig in Hollywood sound like a cross between Attila the Hun and the Marquis de Sade in a court of law, you show an amazing inability to verbalize your own anger," she said, her own slow-to-boil temper clearly flaring. "Now, who exactly are you mad at? Me? Mom? Brandon? The whole damned world?"

Kate winced, not so much at Ellen's furious tone, but at the evident hurt behind it. "I'm not mad at anyone," she said stiffly.

"Oh?" her sister retorted with obvious skepticism. "I have asked you to have dinner with us at least a dozen times since Mom's wedding. You've found an excuse every time, most of them so flimsy they're embarrassing."

Kate refused to meet her sister's gaze. "I'm very busy. You know that."

"Right. But you've always found time for family before. You were the one who went crazy every single time you couldn't get Mother on the phone. You dropped everything, insisted I meet you and went tearing over there. Then that time I called you when I was worried about Mother after she and Brandon had a falling out, you showed up within minutes. You even canceled some big tennis match."

"That was different."

"How?"

"She's our mother, for heaven's sake. And we didn't know what was going on. Her phone was off the hook for hours that one time. Then when you called, you made it sound as if she were about to leap off the top of a skyscraper. That's hardly the same as some casual dinner invitation."

Hurt flared again in Ellen's eyes. "I'm family, dammit. Didn't it occur to you that I might need you?"

Kate couldn't help thinking about David's withdrawal from Davey at a time when he'd been desperately needed. She recalled her own impatience with that behavior. Wasn't she guilty of the same thing? Still, even though she felt ashamed of her selfish behavior, she regarded her sister evenly.

"Are you still family?" she said softly, hearing the unspoken torment behind that simple question, but unable to hide any longer the fact that she felt as if she'd been cast adrift.

Ellen looked as if she'd been slapped. "How could you even ask such a thing?"

"Because it seems to me that you have a new family now. You, Mom and Brandon. That's where you should be spending all your energy, not worrying about me."

For the first time Kate could ever recall, Ellen looked utterly defeated. "Do you think all of this has been easy on me?" she whispered. "My life's been turned upside down, the same way yours has. More so, in fact." She regarded Kate miserably. "Don't you see? I finally understand why all those years we were growing up I felt that Dad loved you more."

Astonishment and dismay swept through Kate. "I had no idea," she said, stunned by her sister's admission. "Dad always treated us the same."

"No," Ellen said angrily. Then she drew in a deep breath. "Oh, he tried. I know that. But I saw the way he looked at you. I could see how proud he was of everything *you* accomplished. It hurt, Katie, especially because I didn't know why I was never good enough."

Reluctant sympathy made Kate's heart ache, but she couldn't cope with Ellen's old wounds now. Her own were still too fresh. She knew she had to get away before she made an absolute fool of herself by bursting into tears—for herself and for her sister and the past that had come between them. She threw her napkin onto the table and stood up. "I'm sorry, Ellen. I can't talk about this anymore right now."

"Kate," Ellen pleaded.

"Not now. I'm sorry," she said, squeezing her sister's hand, hoping Ellen could find some way to understand, some way to forgive her.

She fled, leaving Ellen staring after her, her eyes shimmering with unshed tears.

Outside, Kate muttered a curse over the lack of a car, then decided it was just as well. Maybe on the walk back to Century City the solitude and exercise would clear her head. She knew that she had hurt Ellen, but she hadn't been able to stop herself. All of the pain of feeling like an outsider had boiled over under her sister's attempt at kindness.

Kate didn't want Ellen's pity. She didn't want anyone's pity. She just wanted a family of her own again. Knowing that Ellen might have subconsciously felt that way for years only made the anguish greater.

When she stormed back into the office, not one bit calmer than she had been when she'd left the restaurant, Zelda was on the phone. She quickly hung up and followed Kate into her office.

"I hope you're satisfied," Zelda said, staring at her indignantly. "That was your sister. You left her in tears."

Kate regarded Zelda coldly. "My personal life is none of your concern."

Her secretary's eyes widened at the sharply spoken reminder, but at least she clamped her mouth shut, whirled and walked out.

Terrific, Kate thought. Now Zelda was mad at her, too. How many people could she manage to alienate in one day? And what else could possibly go wrong? When her phone buzzed, she snatched it up and growled a greeting.

"Uh-oh," David said. "Did I catch you at a bad time?"

She drew in a deep breath. She was disgustingly glad to hear his voice, even though she should be furious with him. He'd promised to call the week before about arranging that studio tour for Davey. He hadn't. Even so, she wasn't up to challenging him about it right now.

"Sorry," she said wearily. "It's been a bad day."

"Tough case?" he inquired sympathetically.

Kate almost laughed. If she told him the real reason for her foul mood, he'd question whether she had any business at all setting up rules and regulations for anyone's family life.

"No," she responded finally. "Just a family matter."

"No problem with the honeymoon couple, I hope."

"No. They're fine as far as I know. Look, I really don't want to talk about this," she said dismissively. "Did you have a reason for calling?"

"I did, but it seems my timing's a little off. I was hoping to lure you out to the studio. My schedule's pretty jammed up. That's why I haven't gotten back to you before now. I was thinking maybe tomorrow or the next day. Davey's been bugging me ever since we left your house. Frankly, I think he's more anxious to

see you again than he is to see my sets. I had to promise to call you today. I figured if I didn't, he'd have you
filing more papers."

Kate chafed at the dutiful note in his voice. He
sounded harassed. When he added, "If you can't
make it, I'll understand," she knew he wouldn't just
understand, he'd be grateful for the cop-out.

"Ah, but will Davey?" Kate said wryly.

Even though David sounded as if he'd be just as
happy if she turned him down, Kate couldn't help the
anticipation that swept through her. She glanced at her
calendar. Both days were crammed with appointments. However, she considered Davey's case a pri-
ority. At least, that's what she told herself when she
said, "I think I can clear Wednesday afternoon if we
make it late."

She heard the pages of his appointment book flip.

"How late?" he asked.

"Four-thirty. I know that'll put us smack in the
middle of rush hour when we finish up, but I don't
think I can get out to the valley before then."

"I guess that would work," he said slowly. After
another beat, he added, "We could have dinner after-
ward, so you won't have to worry about the traffic
heading home."

Kate caught the slight hesitation in his voice, the
evident strain. Clearly he had mixed feelings about this
entire invitation. She wondered if he would send
Davey back home alone the minute he'd seen the sets
if she didn't intervene and agree to prolong the evening by joining them for dinner.

To be perfectly truthful, though, she wanted to accept for her own sake, as much as Davey's. The lure of those feelings of contentment she'd experienced over the weekend was too powerful to resist. Especially today, she longed to feel that kind of connection to another human being again.

"Dinner would be great," she said. "Now tell me which studio and soundstage. Should I pick up Davey on the way?"

"If you don't mind, that would really help me out," he said, then gave her directions. "I'll be looking forward to it."

"Me, too," Kate said, realizing as she hung up just how much.

Trying to substitute Davey and David for the family she felt she'd lost was a very bad idea, especially since David clearly had misgivings about a simple tour of his set and dinner. She recognized the dangers with every fiber of her being. And yet, at this moment, the prospect of seeing the two of them again definitely brightened an otherwise dreary, depressing day.

From the moment they walked through the door of the huge soundstage on the lot in Burbank late on Wednesday, Kate felt as if she'd wandered into another world. Beside her, Davey's eyes were wide with awe. David, regarding everything with a critical possessive eye, looked as if he was perfectly at home.

"Wow!" Davey said. "Dad, this is totally hot."

That pretty much summed up Kate's own reaction to a landscape so barren, so otherworldly that she expected to be greeted by an alien at any second. "Definitely hot," she echoed.

David glanced at Kate, a smile tugging at his lips. "Do you suppose that means cool?"

"Or awesome," Kate responded.

"I wish they'd hand out translations of current slang at PTA meetings."

"Just go by the look in his eyes," she suggested. "Can't you see how impressed he is by all this?"

David's gaze clashed with hers and sent a little frisson of awareness tripping through her. "And you?"

"I'm a little awed myself," she admitted. "And a little worried. Are you sure you're of this world? You make this look very real, as if you might have been to this place on your last vacation."

"Just research and imagination, I'm afraid." He held out his hand. Kate took it. "Let's go take a look at the spacecraft. I had a field day with all the gadgetry. Even wrangled a trip to NASA headquarters to see what's actually in use in our current spacecraft. There's nothing in here that's beyond the range of scientific possibility."

As Davey raced on ahead of them, David called out, "Careful of the wires."

The floor was crisscrossed with cables, and the air was filled with the sounds of hammering and shouts as construction crews put the finishing touches on the sets inside the cavernous soundstage. Technicians were running checks on the hot spotlights, creating pools of glaring light.

Despite the unfamiliar surroundings, with her hand clasped firmly in David's, Kate felt the same tantalizing sense of belonging again. She was able to shove her worries aside, at least for a time. Perhaps there was something to be said for living in a fantasy world, even one as alien as the one David had created.

As they stepped through the doorway into a shiny, metallic room filled with blinking lights and an intimidating array of controls and levers, she suddenly wished they could launch this stage prop into another dimension where the demands of the real world no longer had a hold over any of them.

David tugged the door closed behind them, and for just an instant, Kate thought her wish might be granted. Then she saw how soberly he was regarding them.

"Now, look, you two," he warned. "I want to remind you that everything you're seeing today is top secret, okay? The producer wants all of this to make a big splash a few weeks from now when production begins. No leaks."

"I promise, Dad," Davey said solemnly. "Can I push these buttons?"

"Go for it," David agreed with a laugh.

Suddenly they were inundated with shrieking buzzers and clanging bells. The strobe lights flashed with blinding intensity. The noisier and brighter it got, the happier Davey looked.

"It's like being inside a computer game," he announced excitedly.

"Just wait until you see the special effects," David told him. "The man doing them is the best in the business." He watched as Davey touched every surface, fingered every button, then asked, "Think your pals will like it when they see it on-screen?"

Though his tone was casual, Kate detected a hint of insecurity in his eyes. Whether he was willing to admit it or not, he wanted Davey's approval every bit as much as Davey sought his. Her heart ached over the distance between them, an emotional gap that never should have happened between father and son.

Just as it never should have happened between sisters, she thought sadly.

"They'll love it," Davey declared. "Do you think someday I could maybe bring them here?"

"After we've finished shooting the movie," David suggested. "How's that?" He glanced at Kate and seemed to reach a decision of some sort. "You'll have a birthday around that time. Maybe we could have the party here."

Davey could barely contain his excitement. "You promise?"

After an instant of unmistakable uncertainty, David rested his hand on his son's shoulder. "That's a definite promise."

As Davey went exploring again, Kate studied David intently, marveling at his change in mood since they'd talked on the phone on Monday. Then, he'd seemed almost reluctant to see her again, so much so that she'd been certain he'd had second thoughts.

Apparently he caught her scrutiny and somehow guessed the cause. "Kate, I'm sorry about the other day."

"Oh?" she said, not wanting to give any hint that she was even aware of the distance in his voice when they'd talked.

"Things were crazy around here. I couldn't see how I could fit this in at all, but Davey was bugging me." He gazed at her. "I shouldn't have called when I was feeling pressured. I'm sure it sounded as if this were the last thing in the world I wanted to do."

"You didn't sound overly enthusiastic," she admitted.

"I'm sorry. I just want you to know it didn't have anything to do with you or the things I said at the beach. Forgiven?"

"There's nothing to forgive."

His gaze locked with hers. "You sure?"

She smiled slowly. "I'm sure."

He grinned. "Terrific. Now how about some dinner? I promised you food, and you look as if you're faint with hunger."

"It's not that bad," she responded with a laugh, suddenly feeling more carefree than she had in days. "But I did miss lunch so I could take off early this afternoon."

"So what appeals to you when you're starving? Italian? Steak? Seafood? Mexican?"

"Hamburgers," Davey chimed in as he joined them.

"Hey, this is Kate's choice, remember?"

Davey's face fell. Then he glanced at her slyly. "I'll bet she likes hamburgers, too."

"Actually, I do," she confessed. "How about Hamburger Hamlet?"

David shook his head. "And I was prepared to pop for something outrageously expensive."

She grinned at him. "I'll hold you to that another time. Right now this sounds like heaven."

"Okay, then. The one on Beverly Boulevard?"

"Perfect. It's right on the way home."

Davey tucked himself into her side. "Can I ride back with you, too?"

"Actually, I'd like to hitch a ride, too," David said, his expression all innocence, his mood once more bordering on that wicked, flirtatious tone of their weekend at the beach. "I had one of the assistants drop me off here this afternoon."

Kate's eyebrows rose. "And what would you have done if I'd had to take off and left you stranded?"

He grinned back at her. "There's always Mrs. Larsen. Or Dorothy."

"Mrs. Larsen hates to drive all the way out here, Dad," Davey reminded him. "She gets real nervous on the freeways, and she gets lost on the other roads."

"True, but she'd do it in an emergency."

Kate chuckled. "And you consider the failure of a sneaky attempt to hitch a ride in my car an emergency?"

"No, but I would probably suffer irreversible psychological damage if you'd ducked out and left me, and *that* would be an emergency. Besides, you agreed to dinner and I doubt you go back on your promises."

Kate caught the subtle message and gave him a wry look. There was a decidedly wicked twinkle in his eyes as he gazed back at her. Whatever reservations he'd had about this outing had clearly been shoved aside.

"You're a fraud," she accused as she led the way past row after row of huge, tan soundstages to her car. "You've been angling to get behind the wheel of my car from the minute you saw it in the driveway up in Malibu. Admit it."

His expression brightened at once in a way that reminded her of Davey. "You'll let me drive?"

"By all means," she said, handing him the keys. "You won't see any evidence of its power and speed in bumper-to-bumper traffic, but enjoy yourself. Davey and I will squeeze into the passenger seat."

"You do realize, then, how ludicrous and impractical a car like this is in Los Angeles?" he said as he smoothed a hand over the bright red finish. "I don't think anyone's been able to drive over twenty on the freeway in years."

"It's not quite that bad, but what about your car? I suppose you consider that tank practical?" she countered. "When was the last time you needed four-wheel drive to get to the office?"

He laughed. "Touché."

They continued to battle wits over dinner. By dessert Kate had almost forgotten the lousy way the week had started. She even pushed to the back of her mind the guilt that had been nagging at her ever since she'd walked out on Ellen. She needed time to get used to the idea that Ellen understood firsthand what Kate was going through now. She hoped an end to the estrangement was in sight. She would find some way to make it happen—to apologize to her sister.

By the time she dropped her companions off at David's office, her spirits were higher than they had been since their weekend in Malibu. And she was increasingly confident that Davey and David were beginning to rebuild their old rapport. Life, she decided, was not half-bad. She hummed happily all the way home.

Then she opened the door to her apartment and discovered her mother and Brandon in her living room. Though they both looked tanned and relaxed, they did not seem like the ecstatic couple she'd been hearing from for weeks now. And judging from the concerned looks they instantly shot her way, their unhappiness was directly related to her. For an instant she almost regretted having given a spare key to her mother.

When she caught the distinctive scent of raspberry tea, she knew things were serious. That's what her mother always brewed especially for Kate…and only in emergencies.

Chapter Ten

So much for that exhilarating mood she'd been in when she'd left David, Kate thought regretfully. She stifled a groan and plastered a welcoming smile on her face instead.

"Hello, Mother," she said, dropping a kiss on her mother's cheek. "Brandon. You look terrific, but what on earth are you two doing here? Last I heard you were headed for Florence or Paris or someplace."

Brandon shrugged, his sharp gaze studying her intently. Kate detected no anger in the look, just worry.

"Your mother seemed to feel we were needed here," he explained.

"But why?" Kate asked guiltily. "We just talked, a little over a week ago. Everything's fine here."

"No, it is not," her mother said. Those blue eyes of hers sparked indignantly. "You and Ellen are on the outs, and I want to know why."

Kate regarded her with dismay. "She called and told you that? Why would she deliberately set out to ruin your honeymoon?"

"She didn't deliberately set out to do anything. I called. She was upset. Penny got on the phone and with some urging on my part, she finally explained why. I had no idea you and Ellen were quarreling, and over my marriage of all things."

Kate poured herself a stiff drink, then glanced at them. "Want one?"

Brandon shook his head and looked at her mother. "Lizzy?"

"No," she said impatiently. "I want to know what is going on between my daughters."

When Kate remained stonily silent, Brandon stood up and walked over to where she was staring out the window, her back to the room. He put his hand on her shoulder and squeezed. Tears sprang to her eyes, but she blinked them away, praying he wouldn't see them. As much as she wanted to dislike Brandon Halloran, it seemed he wasn't going to let her.

"Kate, you know I'd do anything in the world to make your mother happy, but this is one thing I can't do. You're the only one who can tell her what's wrong and what we can do to help. I hope you will," he said so gently and with such genuine compassion that Kate felt like a spoiled brat for hurting them. How had she allowed things to get so out of hand? Had she secretly wanted her mother to come home as proof she still cared? Lord, she hoped she wasn't that selfish.

She sensed that Brandon had gone back to her mother's side, heard a low murmur of conversation and then the sound of her front door closing.

"Darling," her mother said quietly.

Kate turned and saw the look of anguish on her mother's face. She saw something else as well: understanding.

"Darling, I know you're feeling left out," she said, proving that with a mother's intuition she had guessed what was at the root of Kate's uncharacteristic behavior. It also explained why she had turned up here, rather than at Ellen's. "What can I do to show you that you are still very much a part of my life and of this family?"

Tears spilled freely down Kate's cheeks. "Look, I know this is ridiculous," she said, brushing irritably at the tears. "I'm a grown woman. I shouldn't be so hung up on things staying the way they always were."

Her mother smiled. "Oh, Kate, you always were too hard on yourself. Change is always hard to accept at first. Why do you think it took me so long to say yes to Brandon, even when I loved him with all my heart? I knew how it would disrupt all our lives."

"But you have a right to be happy," Kate insisted, voicing the rational thought that had struggled with her emotional reaction from the outset.

"Yes, I do, but not at the expense of my girls." Her mother shook her head. "I thought Ellen was the one who'd have trouble with this, not you. I should have thought more about how you would feel. You think I betrayed your father, don't you?"

"No," Kate said, too quickly, judging from her mother's skeptical expression. She considered the question more carefully, then repeated her answer. "No. Not really. You and Dad were open with each other. He knew how you felt." She looked at her mother. "He did, didn't he?"

"Yes, and he understood. Darling, your father was a wonderful man, a good father, and I am very sorry he is gone. We had a happy life together, and because of him, I have you. That alone would have made our marriage worthwhile."

Kate sighed and felt some small measure of relief steal through her. "I really needed to hear you say that," she admitted.

"Oh, baby," her mother whispered, her voice catching. "How could you possibly doubt how much I love you?"

Those words echoed sentiments she'd heard from David only days before, the same mix of disbelief and anguish and gut-deep caring of a parent. The parallels between his situation with Davey and her own experience were stronger than she'd realized. And she, like Davey, wanted nothing more than reassurance that their world was still secure. It seemed even someone as self-assured as she was would never outgrow that need to feel connected, loved.

Her mother held her arms wide and Kate stepped into them. The hug, combined with the words, reassured her of something she never should have doubted. Even though Ellen was the child of her mother's love for Brandon Halloran, there was still room in her generous heart for Kate. There always would be.

When their tears were dried and her mother had made another pot of raspberry tea, Kate said, "Now tell me about this fantastic honeymoon, Mom. When are you going to take off again?"

"We don't have a set plan. I think we should stick around here for a while, though."

Kate regarded her with renewed guilt. "Not on my account, please. I'm fine now."

"Are you really, Kate? I'm beginning to think Brandon's right. You need a focus in your life, something more than work. You need a husband."

"I need a trip to the French Riviera more." The snappy retort didn't pack the conviction it might have a week or two ago. Her mother clearly caught the change.

"So," she said casually. "Tell me again about the man who was out at the beach house for the weekend."

Kate regarded her suspiciously. "What have you heard?"

"Heard?" her mother said innocently. "You told me yourself he was the father of a client."

"And you immediately dismissed him as being too old for me. What's changed? I can tell by that gleam in your eyes that you've heard something."

"Actually, I believe Zelda did fax an item over to Rome."

"An item?" Kate said blankly. "What item?" Then she recalled the square clipped out of the middle of one of the trade papers the week before. Zelda had been amazingly evasive when she'd asked about it.

"It mentioned that you and David Winthrop were seen dining together at Alice's along with his son."

"I told you that much."

"No."

"Well, I told you they were at the house."

"You didn't tell me the man's name, dear. If you had, I would have known that the man you were entertaining is one of Hollywood's most eligible bachelors."

"How would you know a thing like that?" Kate demanded, knowing that her mother paid very little attention to the film industry.

"Actually, Brandon made a couple of phone calls," she announced cheerfully. "He seemed quite impressed."

Kate covered her face with her hands. Oh, dear Lord. It was her worst nightmare come true. "Mother, call him off," she begged.

Her mother regarded her smugly. "I don't think so, dear. You're inclined to drag your heels about these things. I think this time, perhaps, you could use a little nudge."

"No nudges," Kate protested. "No meddling. No circumspect investigations. Please."

She could tell from her mother's expression, however, that her pleas were falling on deaf ears. She figured she and David had about another twelve hours while Brandon recovered from jet lag. After that, she suspected there would be no holds barred. Dear heaven, what had she let the man in for?

The definite chill in Kate's office had nothing to do with the air-conditioning. Zelda had been in a snit for over two weeks and, Kate was forced to admit, for good cause. She owed her an apology. Now that her personal life was getting back on a more even keel, it was past time she gave her one.

The door opened and Zelda stood framed in the doorway. "Mrs. Mason is here," she announced without setting foot over the threshold. Her voice held that same distant, icy note that had been giving Kate shivers since the previous week.

"I'll see her in a minute," Kate said. "Come in. I'd like to speak to you."

Zelda took one cautious step inside.

"All the way in," she said dryly. "And close the door."

Zelda reacted as if she were being asked to sign her own death warrant.

"Oh, for goodness' sake," Kate said impatiently. "I'm not going to fire you."

"There are worse things than being fired," Zelda replied huffily.

"Like being yelled at when you were only trying to help?"

Her secretary's eyes widened. "For starters," she said.

"I'm sorry," Kate apologized. "I've been a mess ever since Mom's wedding. I can't really explain why, but that's no excuse for taking it out on you."

"You mean because you and Ellen are only half sisters?"

With a sinking sensation in the pit of her stomach, Kate regarded her in astonishment. "How in the world did you know that?"

"Your sister explained."

Irritation flashed through Kate, followed almost at once by resignation. It was Ellen's story to tell or to keep secret. Obviously she'd needed an ally in her battle to get past Kate's hostility and had trusted Zelda enough to share the information with her. As thrown as she might be feeling at this instant, Kate knew that Ellen's trust had not been misplaced. For all of her off-beat personality, Zelda was as loyal and discreet as she was compassionate.

"I see," Kate said slowly. "Then you understand why I've been unusually stressed out."

Zelda shook her head. "Not really. But if you were feeling so bummed out, why didn't you just talk about it?"

Why, indeed, Kate thought. Wasn't that the advice she parceled out almost hourly to her clients before she agreed to handle a divorce? Wasn't that what she'd been advocating that David and Davey do? Talk out their problems, discuss what was on their minds honestly, and when that didn't work, keep talking until it cut through the barriers. She tried to analyze her reluctance to follow her own advice.

Perhaps it had something to do with a lifetime of feeling in control, of feeling absolute certainty about her place in the scheme of things. She'd always credited her parents for giving her that kind of self-confidence by creating a secure environment, filled with love. The discovery that her world was not at all what she'd thought it to be had caused her to question everything about how she fit in. Nothing had prepared her for the loneliness and desperation of that kind of uncertainty.

The blow had also thrown into doubt everything in her universe. Subconsciously she'd apparently put family on a back burner in order to pursue her career, confident in the stability of their love. When that confidence had been shaken, her priorities had been turned topsy-turvy. Talking about it would only have made it seem more real.

"I guess I was hoping that with time, the feelings would go away," she admitted to Zelda. "I suppose I even felt guilty for begrudging Mom her happiness and Ellen her new father."

Zelda gazed heavenward. "Do you hear that, Lord? The woman is human." She regarded Kate with a shake of her head. "Must have been a rude awakening, huh?"

"You mean Ellen's news?"

"No. I mean discovering that not every single thing in life is within your control."

Kate grinned ruefully. "Yeah," she admitted. "It was. Anyway, I am sorry for taking my mood out on you. Now send Mrs. Mason in."

Zelda nodded. "By the way, Davey called from school. He wants to come by when he gets out. I told him you could fit him in. Okay?"

Kate frowned. "Did he say what it was about?"

"No."

"How did he sound?"

"Like he'd lost his best friend."

Kate muttered a curse and wondered what had happened in the week since she'd last seen Davey and his father. With one of her cases going into court this week, she'd been swamped with preparations and hadn't checked on them. Besides, she'd been so sure that the tension between them was easing and that David understood the importance of rebuilding that relationship. Even as she thought about their fragile rapport and its need for nurturing, it occurred to her that she had some bridges to mend herself.

As if she'd read her mind, Zelda said, "By the way, don't you think you should reschedule that lunch with Ellen?"

"I could almost swear I did not hire you to be my conscience," Kate retorted.

"No," her secretary agreed. "It's a bonus."

Kate laughed. "Call her. Set it up. See if Mom wants to come along."

"Perfect," Zelda said approvingly. "Then maybe she'll relax and finish her honeymoon."

"Is there anything about my family life you don't know?"

"Not much," Zelda said cheerfully. "I'll send Mrs. Mason in."

As it turned out, Mrs. Mason was less in need of legal counseling that she was of a friendly ear for her complaints about the philandering Mr. Mason. Kate suggested she make notes for a tell-all memoir that would embarrass the jerk so badly he'd never want to show his face again at Musso and Frank's, the old film industry hangout on Hollywood Boulevard which had managed to maintain its character despite other changes to the neighborhood. Mrs. Mason's eyes lit up at the suggestion.

"I think I'll buy one of those little tape recorders on the way home," she said, then added with a certain amount of glee, "Just seeing me with one of those ought to terrify him."

Personally Kate thought the bill for a month at a fancy health spa would terrify him more, but clearly Mrs. Mason wanted public revenge more than expensive relaxation.

No sooner had the middle-aged woman gone off in search of a tape recorder than Zelda announced Davey's arrival. To Kate's regret, the boy who walked into her office looked much as he had on his first visit. Too neat. Too polite. Too lonely.

"Hi," she said. "What brings you by?"

"I just wanted to visit," he said in a dull tone. He regarded her uncertainly. "Is that okay?"

"Of course it's okay. My favorite client can always be squeezed in." She watched as he paced the room, looking at pictures, touching the small bronze sculptures she'd chosen as decorations. He seemed particularly fascinated by her Remington cowboy. "How are things at home?" she asked finally.

"Okay, I guess."

"Davey," she said insistently, waiting until he turned to face her. "The truth."

"I thought it was going to be better," he said finally. "I really did. Especially after we went to the beach and everything."

"And the studio," she said.

His chin lifted stubbornly. "But I had to remind him and remind him about that."

"Sweetheart, it was only a week or so after the trip to the beach. Even the very best parents in the whole world can't plan special outings like that for every single day." It was a reasonable excuse, but she could see from Davey's expression that he didn't care about grown-up logic.

"He missed my first ball game, too."

"Did you remind him?"

Davey shrugged and Kate guessed that he hadn't, that he'd wanted his father to come through on his own.

"It's going to take time to work all this out," she told him. "It won't happen overnight."

"I know, but we had a list for all that other stuff. Like breakfast. We were supposed to have breakfast together on the weekends until school started. When I got up Saturday, Dad had gone to the office. Sunday he was out in the yard telling some guy how he wanted him to cut the grass or something. School started Monday, and he hasn't been there for breakfast once." Those brown eyes, which telegraphed his hurt feelings, stared at Kate. "I don't think he likes spending time with me."

Only recently having resolved her own feelings of insecurity, Kate could sympathize, even though she knew he was every bit as wrong about his father as she had been about her family. At least she had been old enough to understand what was going on at an intellectual level, even when she hadn't been able to overcome the hurt. Davey was only ten.

"What would you like me to do?" she asked, wanting him to sense that he had control over the steps she was taking. He needed desperately to believe that at least one grown-up was taking him seriously. Hugs and platitudes wouldn't do it this time.

"Maybe we should go ahead with the divorce."

Kate regarded him seriously, her heart aching for him. "Now let's think about that a minute. Your dad promised to make some changes, didn't he?"

"Yeah, but he's not changing at all."

"No," she corrected, "he did make some. Shouldn't we give him the benefit of the doubt, maybe a little more time?"

"I suppose," he conceded grudgingly. "But then what do we do?"

"I'll talk to him, if you like. I'll remind him that we have a binding, legal agreement, and that he has an obligation to live up to the terms of that agreement."

"But what if he doesn't?"

"Then you and I and he will sit down and discuss the alternatives."

"You mean the divorce," he said dully.

Kate went over and pulled him into a hug. "Sweetheart, I can almost guarantee it will not come to that," she said firmly. Not if there was a way in hell she could prevent it, up to and including personally supervising every single activity David was supposed to be sharing with his son.

"How'd you get here?" she asked Davey.

"Mrs. Larsen brought me. She thinks I went to a movie with my friends, though. I'd better go back over so I'm there when she comes to pick me up." He regarded Kate hopefully. "You'll talk to Dad?"

"Today," she promised. "And I'll call you later."

His expression brightened and he hugged her back finally. "Thanks, Kate."

"You bet, kiddo."

The minute he had left, she buzzed Zelda. "Call David Winthrop and tell him I want to see him in my office." She wanted him on her turf this time. Her *professional* turf, so there could be no mistaking the seriousness of her intentions. This was not a place where they could get sidetracked by easy charm and distracting kisses.

"When?" Zelda asked.

"Today."

"But it's already after four."

"That's okay. I'll wait until he can get here. Don't take no for an answer."

She paced until Zelda buzzed her back.

"He'll be here at six-thirty. Is that okay?"

"Yes. Thanks, Zelda."

"Want me to stick around to take notes?"

"Nope. It won't be necessary," she said, then changed her mind. "Actually, if you don't mind staying, I think it would be a good idea for Mr. David Winthrop to catch on that we're playing for keeps with this."

"I'll wait," Zelda said in a tone that suggested that she was at least as interested in getting a look at David Winthrop as she was in being a dutiful secretary.

David showed up five minutes early. He did not look overjoyed at having been summoned across town at the conclusion of one of the hottest September days on record. He looked mussed and exhausted and irritated. For about ten seconds Kate actually felt sorry for him. Then she remembered why he was there and gathered her resolve. She couldn't let her skittering pulse and sympathetic reaction affect her obligation to Davey.

"Would you mind telling me what is so all-fired important that it couldn't wait until tomorrow?" he demanded. He glared at Zelda, who scowled right back at him. "And what is she doing in here?"

"She's here to take notes. I want this conversation on the record."

He glowered at her. "For what?"

"So I can demonstrate to the court that there was an attempt at mediation."

"The court?" he repeated incredulously. "Have you lost your mind?"

Despite her determination to remain objective and impersonal, she couldn't help identifying with what he must be feeling. Mixed in with the anger was no doubt a good bit of humiliation at having his relationship with his son under public attack. Figuring she'd made her point about the seriousness of the situation, she glanced at Zelda. "You can go. I'll make notes and you can type them up tomorrow."

"Are you sure?"

Kate nodded. When Zelda had gone, she looked at David. "I hope you appreciate the fact that I shouldn't have done that. I thought it might be more constructive, just this once, if you and I talked alone."

"About what?" he snapped, still clearly defensive and obviously feeling besieged. Whatever chemistry had sparked between them in the past appeared to have given way to pure resentment. She couldn't help regretting that and wondering if there would ever come a time when things would be simple.

"We need to discuss your son," she retorted firmly. "Remember him?"

He groaned and sank into a chair. "Not this again." He shoved his fingers through his already tousled hair. "I thought we'd resolved this."

"So did I," Kate said evenly. "Unfortunately, Davey stopped by to see me today. According to him, nothing seems to have changed."

"How can you say that? We spent a whole damned weekend with you. We toured the studio."

Kate winced at his beleaguered tone.

"What the hell do you want?" he demanded. "I'm on a tight deadline. I'm doing the best I can."

Actually, he sounded about at the end of his patience and his energy. Kate's resolve wavered under a flood of empathy. She'd had stretches of weeks, even months, exactly like this, with no time even to pause to catch her breath. She could identify completely with the tension he was obviously under and, for that matter, the choices he had made.

"Are you really trying?" she said, but more gently. She owed it to Davey to get the point across, no matter how much she might relate to David's dilemma.

"Yes, dammit. You have no idea what it's like getting crews to bring this job in on time, dealing with a director who's had a sudden brainstorm that changes the set for one entire scene, handling a producer who's going ballistic over the budget. I'm at the end of my rope here. I don't need you adding to it."

The last of Kate's indignation on Davey's behalf faltered. She looked into David's tired eyes and saw a man just struggling to survive.

"I'm sorry," she said, resisting the urge to walk over and massage away the obvious tension in his shoulders. "But we do have a problem here. Davey doesn't understand all this. All he sees is that you made promises and now you're not keeping them." At the risk of incurring another explosion, she added, "It's not as if he has anyone else at home he can depend on."

His expression went absolutely still. "Don't you think I know that?" he whispered.

He regarded her with such absolute misery that something inside her shifted. She couldn't think of any way to respond that wouldn't jeopardize the stand she had to take for Davey's sake. Instead, she waited and listened as he struggled to find his own way out of the mess.

He started to pace, stopping to finger the same objects that had intrigued Davey only hours earlier. Holding the Remington sculpture, he faced Kate. "I don't know what else I can do, not now, anyway. Once this job is over, I can slow my pace down some, make more time for Davey."

Kate recognized the excuse and the well-meant, but probably empty promise. "Will you do that?" she asked. "Or will you bury yourself in just one more project and then one more after that? I'm familiar with the pattern. I do it myself all the time. It's a great way to avoid living."

He scowled at her. She didn't allow herself to waver, even though she badly wanted to recapture their personal rapport for reasons that didn't bear too much scrutiny under the circumstances. Finally some of the anger eased out of his expression. He regarded her ruefully. "Sounds as if you've been engaging in a little self-discovery yourself lately."

"Painful, but true," she admitted. "Actually, I owe some of it to you. I recognized some of my behavior in what you're doing. They always say recognizing what you're up against is the first step toward change."

He grinned and carefully placed the sculpture back on the credenza. "So you did read those pop psychology books your guests left behind after all?"

"A few," she conceded. "Look, no one knows better than I how difficult it is to choose family over work, but it has come to my attention lately that I've made some lousy choices. Isn't it just possible that you have, too?"

"Oh, I'd say it's a dead-on certainty," he agreed without batting an eye. "But, Kate, that doesn't mean I know how the hell to change, not when I'm in the middle of a professional commitment. If I screw this up, my reputation for being on time and on budget will never be the same. This industry can be unforgiving."

"Surely there's room for compromise." She held up the paper he'd signed. "You make the changes one step at a time," she reminded him. "Isn't that what they say?"

He sighed heavily. "So I've heard."

"We can go over this, modify it so that it's more reasonable, given your commitments for the next few weeks. It's better to give Davey some realistic expectations than to have him constantly disappointed by your failure to live up to these."

As she spoke, she realized that he was studying her intently. She lifted her eyes to his and their gazes locked. Electricity arced between them in sufficient voltage to light a soundstage.

"How about dinner?" he said. "Do you have plans? We could work out these modifications."

Kate wanted badly to accept. She wanted to pursue the sensations that had the atmosphere in the room suddenly charged. She wanted to be held and kissed and . . .

"No," she said with great reluctance. Pleased by his obvious disappointment, she added gently, "You do have plans, though. Go home to your son."

"Could I persuade you to come along?"

"As a buffer? I don't think so."

"I was thinking more as a friend."

Kate's heart seemed to stand still. She knew how badly they both needed a friend right now, but not tonight. Davey came first.

"Because we are friends," she said with an unexpected mixture of certainty and definite anticipation, "there will be other nights."

He nodded finally. "I suppose you're right."

He stood up and Kate walked with him to the elevator. When the doors opened, he leaned down and gave her a quick kiss. The touch of his mouth was warm and feather-light, but it was a commitment nonetheless, a promise that the time was coming when they would explore these fresh, new feelings that were blossoming for both of them even under these trying circumstances.

"Thanks," he said. "Despite my rotten attitude, I know that Davey's fortunate to have you in his corner."

Kate reached up and touched his cheek. "Don't forget that he's lucky to have you for a father, too."

He regarded her ruefully. "I thought you just finished telling me what a lousy job of parenting I was doing."

"Right now," she said gently. "Not always. If you hadn't been such a great father before, he wouldn't be missing you so much now."

"Thank you for saying that," he said. Then, just as the elevator doors slid closed, he added, "I hope you know what an incredibly special woman you are, Kate Newton. I really mean that."

Kate sighed. Thanks to him and Davey and her own family, she was just beginning to remember that she had a worth that extended far beyond her value as an attorney.

Chapter Eleven

When David walked into the house, he found Davey seated alone at the huge dining room table, looking so forlorn that David felt his heart wrench with guilt and dismay. No little boy should ever look that sad.

"Hey, pal," he said. His breath caught at the expression of happiness that instantly brightened his son's face. How had he forgotten that this was what mattered? How had he lost sight of the wonder of having Davey regard him with such open adoration?

"Dad! I didn't know you were coming for dinner."

"Sorry I'm late. Where's Mrs. Larsen?"

"In the kitchen. She wanted to watch the news and her game shows. Sometimes I watch with her, but it's pretty boring. I told her I wanted to eat in here."

"By yourself? Why not in the den, so you could watch a video or something?"

"Mrs. Larsen says the den's no place for food. That's why we have a kitchen and a dining room," he said in a tone that precisely mimicked the housekeeper's.

Suddenly angrier than he had been in a very long time, David forgot about his own meal. He pulled out a chair and sat down. He studied his son's neatly combed hair, the spotless shirt he was wearing. He'd always assumed such things were an indication of what good care the woman was taking of his son. Now he realized what Kate had meant when she'd told him weeks earlier that the housekeeper was rigid, even though she clearly cared a great deal for Davey.

"What else does Mrs. Larsen say?" he said tightly.

"She says lots of stuff," Davey said with a shrug. "She has rules for just about everything. I'll bet she never had any fun when she was a kid."

"How about shooting some baskets with me?" David said impulsively. Suddenly he badly wanted to see his son flushed with excitement and messed up from having exactly the sort of fun Davey assumed the housekeeper had missed in her childhood.

"Now?" Davey replied, his eyes lighting up. He glanced at the generous scoop of baby carrots and broccoli untouched on his plate and his face fell. "I haven't finished my vegetables. Mrs. Larsen says beta...beta-something is an important vitamin."

"To hell with your vegetables," David said, thinking that Mrs. Larsen said entirely too much. "Let's go."

Davey started for the stairs.

"Where are you going?"

"I have to change into my play clothes."

"You do not," David said firmly, as he unbuttoned his shirt and tossed it on the dining room chair. Fortunately he was wearing jeans and sneakers. "Not tonight, anyway. Where's the basketball?"

"In the garage."

"Good. I'll get it and switch on the outside lights." He grinned at his son. "I hope you've been practicing, because I'm feeling very lucky tonight."

Davey giggled as he darted past him. "Dad, you're terrible, except at free shots."

"Terrible?" David retorted indignantly. "I'll show you terrible, you ungrateful little monster."

They thundered through the kitchen, startling Mrs. Larsen, whose mouth immediately turned down into a disapproving frown. She opened her mouth, but before she could say a word, David gazed at her evenly and said, "You and I will have a talk later. I think some changes are in order around here."

Eyes wide with astonishment and instantaneous anxiety, she stared after him. David felt only minimally guilty for disrupting her meal and her routine. He felt worse about making her anxious. Though his first ill-tempered instinct had been to fire her, he realized that would be unfair.

Over the years Mrs. Larsen had been good to all of them. In fact, she had been a real saint during Alicia's illness, treating her as tenderly as if she'd been her own daughter. She was older, and no doubt a firm hand and rigid rules were her way of coping with an energetic boy. Hopefully he could make her see that a more moderate approach of discipline was called for.

As he and Davey played basketball, he realized exactly how much his son had improved since the last time they'd been on the court. Not only was he quick on his feet, but his shots were increasingly sure, despite whatever pressure David put on him. He was also sneaky as the dickens when it came to blocking his father's shots. They called the game at nine o'clock, when they were tired and sweaty and dead even.

"Enough," David cried, collapsing onto the grass beside the half court that backed up to the garage.

"Chicken," Davey accused. "I had the ball. One more minute and I would have won."

"Probably so," David conceded with a laugh, wondering how his son had developed such a fierce competitive streak. Kate would no doubt say the boy had inherited it from him. But he hadn't always been that way. He'd only become driven since Alicia's death. Perhaps with Kate and Davey prodding him, to say nothing of Dorothy, he could get his priorities back in order.

He ruffled Davey's damp hair. "Think how humiliating it would have been for me to lose. Give your old man a break."

"You want a drink?" Davey asked. "I could bring us a pop."

"Wonderful," he said gratefully.

When Davey returned with the cans, he sat down next to his father. "I think Mrs. Larsen is really worried," he said, sounding genuinely concerned about the housekeeper. "You're not really mad at her, are you, Dad?"

"No, not really. I just want to talk to her about relaxing a few rules around here."

"Good," Davey said, "'cause she's not so bad. It's not like she's really mean."

David regarded his son proudly. "You're a great kid to stand up for her."

Davey shrugged. "She's not like a mom or anything," he said carefully. "But she bakes pretty good cookies and stuff, and she'll usually take me places to see my friends. I think it makes her nervous, though, when they come here. She's afraid we're all going to fall in the pool and drown."

"Is that why you don't have your friends over so much?"

It was a long while before Davey answered. "Not really," he said.

"Why, then?"

"I like to go to their houses better," he admitted finally.

David thought of the way his own home had always been the center of his boyhood activities. He'd wanted that for Davey, too. He wondered why it hadn't happened that way. Then he recalled the way things had been during Alicia's illness, how quiet they'd tried to keep things for her. Had Davey stopped inviting his friends over then? Or was the answer as uncomplicated as the choices of entertainment available in his friends' homes?

"Do they have more stuff to do?" he asked, though he couldn't imagine any child having more toys than his son.

Davey shook his head, his gaze focused determinedly on a smudge on his sneakers. He rubbed it intently.

Puzzled by Davey's sudden reticence, David prodded, "Son, what is it?"

Those huge brown eyes that could break his heart finally met his.

"Most of them have a mom and a dad," he said wistfully. "It's really nice."

The pain that cut through David then was worse than any heart attack, worse than the anguish he'd felt the day Alicia had died. He reached over and gathered Davey close. Skinny arms circled his neck, the rare gesture all the more precious coming from his too-big-for-hugs son.

"I'm sorry, Davey," he whispered, his throat clogged with emotion. "God, I'm so sorry."

After a while he felt tears fall onto his chest, but he had no way of knowing if they were Davey's or his own.

David got Davey into bed, then showered, put on pajama bottoms and a robe for Mrs. Larsen's sake and went in search of the housekeeper. He found her in her room, still dressed, still looking as if she feared dismissal.

"Mrs. Larsen, I apologize if my behavior earlier worried you."

"I try to make allowances," she said primly, following him into the kitchen. She pulled out a chair and sat down heavily, obviously expecting the worst.

David wondered guiltily how many allowances had been made in the months since Alicia had died and the burden for caring for his house and his son had fallen on Mrs. Larsen's sturdy shoulders.

"You've done a wonderful job around here," he reassured her. "I really don't know what I would have done without you. But I am concerned about Davey."

The relief that had flickered in her eyes gave way to defensiveness. "What's he been telling you?"

"Nothing, I promise you. I just have the feeling that perhaps it's time we were a little more lenient with him. He needs to learn to take responsibility for his actions. I think you've laid a solid foundation for that, don't you?"

"But he's still just a boy," she protested. "He needs guidance."

"Exactly. He needs guidance, not military discipline. Perhaps we could loosen the rules just a little. If I'm not home, for example, and he wants to eat in his room or the den, I think a tray could be prepared, don't you?"

Though she looked horrified by the very thought, she nodded. "I suppose, though there's bound to be a mess."

"Then he'll have to clean it up."

She gave an approving bob of her head. "I suppose that would do."

"And I'd like you to encourage him to invite his friends here. I know it's asking a lot. Ten-year-old boys tend to be noisy and rambunctious, but I think it's only reasonable that Davey pay them back for having him over so often. I'll try to make sure that I'm home when they're here, too."

An idea from his own childhood occurred to him. "Maybe next weekend he could even have a sleep-over, if you wouldn't mind baking an extra couple of batches of those cookies he likes so much. I'll order in pizza and soft drinks."

The prospect of the deafening commotion a group of ten-year-olds could create was almost as daunting for him as it was for Mrs. Larsen, but he was determined that she not be the only one making changes around here. He would try to manage some without Kate's insistence, though he couldn't deny he wanted her approval.

Mrs. Larsen's gaze softened just a little. "If you don't mind my saying so, sir, I think that's what he really needs, a bit more of your attention."

"So I've been told," David said ruefully. "That's all for tonight, Mrs. Larsen. If you run into any problems, please talk them over with me."

"Yes, sir," she said. She started back for her room, then turned around. "It's good to see you taking an interest again, Mr. David."

He sighed. "Thank you, Mrs. Larsen. I should have done it long ago."

When she had gone, he went into his den and sank into the wing chair where he'd found Kate a few weeks earlier. For the first time in ages, he was pleasantly worn out, rather than gut-deep exhausted. He also saw how right she'd been about how much Davey needed him. He'd have to tell her that the next time they spoke.

Why not tonight? Impulsively he picked up the phone, glanced at the card attached to the legal papers Kate had given him and dialed her number. The service picked up.

"Is it urgent, Mr. Winthrop?"

He figured it was at least as urgent as her demand to see him earlier. "Yes."

"I'll have her call you."

It was less than five minutes before his phone rang. The smoky sound of Kate's voice made his heart leap in a way that was altogether astonishing. It seemed when she wasn't infuriating him, she was turning him on.

"I wanted to thank you," he said, even as he listened to the unspoken explanation for the call echoing inside him: *I wanted to hear your voice.*

"For what?"

"For the best night I've had in a long while." *For caring.*

"With Davey?" she said.

"Yes." *And with you.*

"I'm so glad." There was a note of genuine happiness in her voice. "What'd you do?" she asked, as if she were eager to hear every single detail.

"Played basketball until we dropped."

"Who won?"

"No one. I had sense enough to call the game when we were tied."

"You mean before he beat you?" she taunted.

"That's what he said," he grumbled. "I think you two are in cahoots."

"Yes, we are," she admitted with a laugh.

David sighed. "I'm glad," he told her. "I can't promise things will change overnight, but I am trying, Kate."

"That's all I can ask."

Suddenly there were so many things he wanted to say to her, so many things he wanted to discover about this woman who'd bulldozed her way into his life. Realizing that he was genuinely beginning to care, he waited for the onset of guilt, but it didn't come. Once more he saw that tonight had been a real turning point in his life. He owed her for that, for opening him up to living again.

"I'll see you soon," he said. He kept to himself the one thing he wanted to say above all others: *I can't wait to hold you in my arms to see if there really are miracles.*

"See you soon," she echoed.

It was a full minute before either of them actually broke the connection, as if they were both reluctant to go back to their own lonely, isolated worlds again.

Even though Kate felt reassured by her meeting with David and his late-night call, she recognized that the changes she was asking for were not likely to happen overnight without a little nudge every now and then. She was very good at nudging.

She started by calling the house every morning at seven o'clock to remind David that he was supposed to stick around to have breakfast with his son. Of course, hearing David's sleepy, sexy voice at that hour of the morning did delightfully wicked things to her frame of mind for the rest of the day, as well.

If David was bothered by her blatant interference, it never once showed in his voice. In fact, the conversations lengthened day by day, touching on their own plans for the day, exploring the latest news. Kate soon felt she knew his schedule almost as well as she knew her own. Too often she found herself glancing at the clock during the day and recalling where he'd said he'd be.

But despite the closeness she was beginning to feel, despite the unexpectedly satisfying warmth of feeling as if she was some small part of his life, neither of them made any overtures to get together. It was just as well, she told herself. Her schedule was jammed from dawn until way past dusk, just as it had always been. It seemed the advice she'd been quick to give him hadn't affected her own behavior at all.

Then, when she'd been calling for just over a week and least expected it, David suggested she stop by and join them for breakfast. "The weather's beautiful on the terrace in the mornings. It's a great way to start the day," he said, as if he'd just made the discovery and couldn't wait to share it.

She was torn between accepting and duty. "I have to be in court at nine."

"Tomorrow, then. It's Saturday. No excuses. Besides, your client asks about you all the time. Could be he's already tired of my company."

She laughed at his deliberate sneakiness. "And I thought I was a master manipulator. Okay, I'll be there. Just promise me that Mrs. Larsen won't make oatmeal. Davey told me it's like cement."

"It could hold buildings together during an earthquake," David agreed. "Okay. No oatmeal. We'll see you about eight."

"Sounds good." She'd started to hang up when she heard his voice.

"Kate?"

"Yes."

"Good luck in court."

She was already feeling exceptionally lucky.

On Saturday with the weatherman calling for record heat again, Kate chose a bright yellow sundress that reflected her cheery mood when she dressed to join David and Davey for breakfast. She spent an extraordinary amount of time on her makeup, assuring herself that it looked natural. The irony of that did not escape her. She spent less time on her hair, knowing that the wind would play havoc with whatever style she attempted. She refused to put the top up on the car just to save a hairdo, especially on a day made for a convertible.

As she drove to David's, her pace leisurely despite the deserted roads, she anticipated the changes in his rapport with his son. She could hardly wait to see how much progress they'd made. Then, uttering a little sigh, she confessed to herself that she could hardly wait to explore the changes she had sensed in her own relationship with David. Every phone call had had an increasingly provocative undercurrent, no matter how mundane the actual topic.

Mrs. Larsen greeted her at the door, her expression perfectly bland, though Kate was almost certain she caught a surprising twinkle in the housekeeper's eyes. Perhaps Mrs. Larsen had a touch of romance in her soul after all.

"Mr. David is on the terrace," she said. "Follow me."

"And Davey?"

"He spent the night at a friend's. I'm not sure exactly what time he's expected back."

Kate's step faltered. Davey wasn't here? Wasn't the whole purpose of this visit to give her a chance to be reassured about how much better he and his father were getting along? She hadn't realized until just that instant how much she had been counting on Davey to provide a buffer between her and his father. His presence would have guaranteed that everything would remain pleasantly impersonal, even if her own common sense had taken a nosedive.

As she followed Mrs. Larsen onto the terrace, David rose to greet her from the table that had been set beside the pool. He was wearing a bathing suit and an unbuttoned shirt. He'd obviously just been for a swim. His hair was curling damply, and droplets of water sparkled on his lightly tanned skin. She found her gaze locking on the very masculine expanse of bare chest as her pulse accelerated faster than her car ever had.

David's gaze swept over her. The expression in his eyes was so warmly appreciative that Kate had to swallow hard against the nervousness that seemed lodged in her throat.

"You look absolutely ravishing," he said softly.

His tone set her pulse off again. To counteract the suddenly provocative tenor the morning was taking, she lifted her chin and regarded him indignantly.

"I thought Davey was going to be here," she said.

"He was, but a friend called last night and invited him over. He really wanted to go."

"Why do I have the feeling you practically shoved him out the door?" she grumbled.

She noticed that he didn't bother trying to deny it.

"Because you know that I've been wanting to be alone with you for quite some time now," he said.

"I don't know that," she argued, futilely hoping to salvage some of the distance that she needed to keep her emotions safe.

"Liar," he accused.

Then, as if he sensed that she might yet bolt, he relented. "Sit down, Kate. Juice and coffee are on the table. Breakfast should be out any minute. We're having French toast stuffed with cream cheese and orange marmalade. I trust that sounds suitably decadent."

Kate's mouth watered. "Decadent? It sounds suicidal."

"We'll swim off the calories," he promised as Mrs. Larsen placed plates laden with delectable-looking food in front of them.

"This many calories?" she asked skeptically.

"We have all day to work them off."

Her gaze darted to the pool and back to him. "I didn't bring a suit."

"Not a problem," he said in a way that sent her imagination running wild. Finally he grinned and added, "There are suits in the pool house, if you really insist on wearing one."

"Oh, I really insist," she muttered breathlessly, though she was more taken than she liked to admit with the idea of skinny-dipping under the blazing sun with this man. She was scandalized by the effect he seemed to be having on her without half trying. What on earth would happen if he ever put his mind to seducing her?

"Kate?" he said softly.

"Yes?" Her fork clattered against the plate as she met his gaze.

"Don't be afraid of what's happening between us."

"Is something happening?" she asked, retrieving the fork and holding it in a deathlike grip.

"I'm not sure when or how it happened, but it is for me. I can see in your eyes that it is for you, too."

Kate wondered just what he was feeling. Lust? He'd probably been celibate for a long time. They'd been thrown together a lot lately, shared a couple of steamy kisses. He'd probably jumped to all sorts of wicked and incorrect conclusions as a result. She tried to give herself time by taking a bite of the food. It was probably delicious. It could just as easily have been sawdust.

"David, I understand that you've been lonely," she began finally.

"This has nothing to do with loneliness," he retorted patiently.

"No. I think it does. It's natural..."

"Yes. It is natural," he interrupted, not allowing her to put another spin on the attraction. "Look, I'm not rushing into anything here. Lord knows, I have been lonely. But I have also fallen in love once before in my life. I know how that feels, too. We discussed this once. Those bells, remember?"

Kate shot a startled, desperate look at him. "Love," she repeated, her voice wavering. She pushed the plate aside. All interest in food had fled. What she needed was a drink. Too bad he hadn't served mimosas. Champagne and orange juice would have smoothed over this jagged nervousness she was feeling.

"Don't panic," he said, his expression amused. "I'm not jumping to any conclusions. I've just made a conscious decision to open myself up to the possibilities."

"You sound like somebody contemplating having their astrological chart done for the first time, part skepticism, part hope."

"Exactly." His smile faded and his gaze clashed with hers. "Can't you at least meet me halfway on this?"

"Halfway?" she repeated, as if there were a spot on the lawn he could pinpoint. She knew she was beginning to sound half-addled, but she wasn't prepared to leap into something even halfway as an experiment. That's how people got badly hurt.

"It's been the obligatory half hour since we finished eating. At least, you haven't touched a bite in that long," he taunted. "We could make that halfway point in the pool."

Kate wasn't wild about getting into a bathing suit or into a pool with a man who'd declared his intention to explore the way he felt about her. But at least a trip to the pool house might give her a few minutes to gather her composure and remind herself—quite sternly, in fact—that she was not in the market for a quick tumble in anyone's bed.

Her body, she noticed with some regret, seemed to have other ideas.

Chapter Twelve

As Kate headed for the pool house to change, David decided he definitely needed a dip in the pool to cool off. For a woman so damned determined not to be provocative, she'd had his temperature rising from the minute she'd strolled onto the terrace looking as cool and refreshing as a tall glass of lemonade.

Of course, he admitted candidly, it was entirely likely that any one of the bathing suits she chose from the supply on hand would be even more disturbing than that dress, which had simply bared her shoulders and swirled around her like a pool of sunlight. Just the anticipation stirred an arousal that not even the cool, turquoise water of the pool could counteract. Clearly it was payback time for months of celibacy. His body was reminding him with throbbing urgency that he was still very much alive.

He started to swim long, hard strokes that had his taut body slicing through the water. He completed one lap, flipped and went back the other way. He'd done nearly twenty exhausting laps, when he finally stopped. Breathless, he clung to the edge of the pool. It was a full minute before he glanced up, saw Kate standing hesitantly before him and felt every nerve ending in his body clamor for just one thing. It wasn't a quick game of water polo.

Dear Lord, what was he about to do? he wondered desperately as his gaze locked on the unrevealing one-piece bathing suit that still managed to entice like the most daring bikini. The sedate neckline didn't dip too low, but that didn't matter. There was no way it could hide the lush fullness of her breasts, something her usual power suits managed to disguise. The cut of the bottom wasn't especially high on the sides, but it still revealed long, shapely legs and hips that were meant to cradle a man. The slick black material fit like a second skin. David's pulse took on a staccato rhythm. He was afraid if she stood there one more instant, his rampaging hormones would lead them both into more trouble than they'd bargained for.

"Dive in," he urged. "The water's wonderful."

"Not too cold?"

Not that he'd noticed, he thought wryly. He shook his head. "Take the plunge."

If she caught the unintended double entendre, she didn't show it by so much as the flicker of an eyelash.

She simply walked to the edge at the deep end, lifted her hands in a diver's stance and cut into the water with barely a ripple to disturb the sparkling surface. Not two seconds later, she came up sputtering, goose bumps already rising on her pale-as-cream skin.

"It's like ice, damn you!" she said and swam toward him with a gleam of mock ferocity in her eyes.

David couldn't help laughing at her indignation. "Just the thing for a hot day, don't you think?"

"It's not hot yet," she pointed out as she drew closer. "Maybe by noon this would feel terrific." As if to emphasize how cold it was, her teeth began to chatter. "S-see what I mean?"

"What you need is a little exercise," he announced. "It'll warm you right up. I'll race you to the end of the pool and back."

"You're on," she agreed with that devilish glint back in her eyes.

She pushed off. The fact that her first kick landed squarely in his midsection was probably just an accident, he told himself as he took off after her.

Kate was good, he realized as he caught her, then found her matching him stroke for stroke. She was also a fighter and she didn't necessarily play fair. More than once she managed to tangle her legs with his just enough to throw him off, while she swam confidently on. When they'd finished two laps, she grinned at him as she executed a tight flip and muttered, "Again?"

She didn't wait for his response. She was a half lap ahead by the time he could reverse directions. He was too much a competitor to lag behind for long, though.

He pushed his endurance to catch and then pass her. Several laps later, they were both clinging to the side trying to catch their breath.

He looked into her eyes and found himself mesmerized by the light shimmering in their depths. That brilliant spark lured like a lantern in the darkness. Without thinking, just reacting to a deep, yearning need, he tucked one hand around the back of her neck and drew her closer. He felt the shiver that raced over her. When his lips claimed hers, she shuddered. He felt her cool skin turn warm under the persuasive touch of his mouth, the gentle teasing of his tongue.

There was an instant as his hand settled at the curve of her hip when her body tensed as if she might push him away. David's breath seemed to lodge in his chest as he waited for her decision. And then, when he wasn't sure he could bear another second of indecision, she relaxed and melted against him. Her hands slid up his chest with slow, teasing deliberation, then locked behind his neck as she turned her head to angle her mouth under his, open to the invasion of his tongue.

David groaned. Her skin was warm and cool at once, the fire inside chilled by the pool's water. Slick with moisture, her body felt the way it might have after long, sensuous hours of lovemaking. As that thought struck him, he wondered that steam didn't rise around them.

His hands skimmed along the material of her bathing suit, learning the shape of her, discovering that the layer of fabric tantalized, even as it thwarted flesh-on-flesh contact. He could feel the hardening of her nipples as he caressed her breasts, could feel the way she seemed to move into his touch, rather than holding back. The subtly sensuous movements almost drove him crazy.

He sensed then that Kate was a woman who would hold nothing back when it came to giving and receiving pleasure. A woman like that would be more vulnerable than most and a great tide of tenderness washed over him when he realized the rare gift she was sharing with him, the risk she appeared willing to take with her own peace of mind.

He framed her face with his hands, his gaze locked on hers, trying to see into her soul. He tried to judge one last time if he had misread things, if she truly was with him all the way on the desires that were throbbing deep inside, crowding out everything else. He saw only a need that matched his own. Whatever doubts she might have about them, about the future—and if he had dozens, she was bound to have more—she had committed herself to following his lead. She seemed more than ready to explore the sensations that were as old as time, yet as sparkling new as if this were the first time in their lives for each of them.

"Kate?" he said softly.

Those dark eyes of hers blazed back at him, filled with life, luring him into a world of powerful need and thrilling sensation, drawing him from the past into the present, into this one, single moment in time. Deep inside, something slowly shifted, eased, freeing him forever from the past, blessing his decision to move on.

He knew, though, that if they ventured further—he and this warm, passionate woman he held—for him there would be no turning back. To him, making love had always been a commitment, a promise, and for reasons he couldn't have explained if he'd tried, he knew that was as true for him now as it had ever been. It didn't seem to matter that Kate was only weeks past being a stranger. It didn't even seem to matter that she was a declared adversary. In fact, he was stunned to discover that it felt so right that his choice this time was Kate, a woman so unlike Alicia. She was harder, more fiercely competitive, more passionate about everything.

And then he looked more deeply into her eyes, those windows to the soul, and saw the anxiety, the well-spring of gentleness, the yearning. So, he thought, as he captured her mouth once more, it wasn't so surprising after all.

The surprise came when he carried her from the pool and, still dripping wet, into the master bedroom suite. It came when she declined slow, gentle touches and set a pace that was just shy of desperate, a frenzied claiming that left them in a tangle of wet bathing suits and pushed them into a fevered, urgent release that rocked the bed and left them both gasping for breath.

"Dear Lord," he said, when he could finally gather breath to say anything at all.

Kate, her hair a dark tangle against the pillow, her skin flushed and damp, merely smiled. It was a contented Mona Lisa smile. Had she been a cat, David thought with amusement, she would have been purring. Even her slow, lazy, sensuous stretch spoke of satisfaction and bore no hint of the self-consciousness she had displayed earlier. This Kate was all woman and reveling in it.

"It occurs to me that you should wear a tag warning of danger," he teased, still pleasantly startled by her complete and generous sharing of her body. "I'm stunned."

"I must admit to being a little stunned myself," she said, laughing with him. "Two hours ago I would have sworn that I didn't want this to happen, that I wouldn't allow it to happen."

Having felt much the same way, David circled his arms around her and settled her against his chest. He smoothed her hair away from her face. "What happened to change your mind?"

He felt the slight shake of her head.

"I'm not sure," she said, her breath whispering against his overheated flesh. "Suddenly it just felt right, as if it would be absolutely foolish to resist when I wanted to be held like this more than anything."

"By me?"

Her gaze, filled with surprise, met his. "Of course by you." She pulled away and she studied him more intently. "What about you? Is this what you had in mind when you lured me over here?"

David searched his heart for the answer to that. The quick, easy answer was no. The truth seemed much more complicated. "Although I've denied it for weeks now, I think I've wanted you from the first moment I set eyes on you."

"You thought I was an uppity bitch when you first laid eyes on me," she reminded him.

"Always the biggest challenge," he retorted, chuckling at the indignation that flared in her eyes. He touched her lips, which were threatening to curve into a smile despite her best efforts to stop herself. "Ah, Kate, you've made me laugh again."

"And yell," she said. "Don't forget the yelling."

He pressed a kiss against her forehead. "The point is you've made me feel things again. For a very long time, I wasn't sure that was possible."

She sighed and settled more comfortably in his arms. "Right this instant, almost anything seems possible."

"Yes," he murmured. "It does."

He heard her breathing slow into a quiet, steady rhythm. He swept a hand down her spine, stopping eventually on the curve of her bottom. He was fascinated by the unexpectedly easy intimacy between them. He'd expected if the time ever came when he brought another woman to this bed, he would be battling ghosts.

Perhaps that explained Kate's aggressive, urgent lovemaking, he thought with sudden understanding. She hadn't wanted him to have time to think. She had wanted him so caught up in what was happening be-

tween the two of them, in the perfect fit of their bod-
ies, in the demanding need, that there was no time for
second thoughts. If that had indeed been her intention, he owed her for making this step easier for him
to take.

"Ah, Kate," he murmured, even though she wasn't
awake to hear him. "You are, perhaps, the most en-
chanting, complex woman I have ever known."

How the hell was she supposed to extricate herself
from this mess, Kate wondered when she awoke. She
was not thinking of the tangled sheets and bathing
suits currently holding her captive in this bed, either.
She was referring to the fact that she had ignored her
best intentions and behaved like an absolutely wan-
ton woman the very first time David Winthrop had so
much as given her a come-hither glance.

Okay, so it had been more than a glance. It had been
a couple of those bone-melting kisses, but the point
was the same. Her resolve, based on pretty sound, rational thought, had vanished like a puff of smoke.
Poof! Gone! And she'd convinced herself that she was
a woman ruled by her intellect rather than her hormones, she thought wryly. What a joke that was.

She blinked open one eye and dared a glance at the
man against whom she was currently snuggled up. He
was drop-dead handsome, she thought with a sigh.
And sexy. Even now, when regrets were stampeding
through her at a hundred miles an hour, she wanted
him. She wanted him to look at her the way he had
earlier, as if she were the most desirable woman on the

face of the earth. She wanted him to touch her again with that mixture of reverence and fascination that turned suddenly urgent. She wanted to be swept away on a tide of glorious, magical sensation one more time.

And then she wanted to go home and pretend it had never happened, wipe it from her mind, go on living as if something cataclysmic hadn't just happened to her. It was very important that she be able to do that, too. She didn't have a doubt in the world that a man who hadn't been able to push grief aside for the sake of his beloved son was hardly ready to embrace a new relationship.

As for her, everyone knew she had chosen to go through life alone. It was less complicated, less hurtful. There might be a real shortage of peaks, but there definitely were no miserable valleys, either. She'd plunged into the lowest valley of them all with Ryan and vowed never again.

She stroked her fingers along David's smooth jaw. It was too bad it had to be this way, she thought regretfully. The peak they had just attained without half trying had been one damned fine peak.

She closed her eyes and wished they could linger this way forever, suspended in time. Suddenly she felt him nuzzling against her, felt his mouth, warm and wet, surround her nipple. The deep, sucking sensation sent a live current jolting through her. Regrets fled. Common sense fled. Only need, sweet and wild, sliced through her as she felt her body waken beneath his slow, lazy caresses.

Hands roughened, probably by one too many close encounters with chain saws, skimmed over her flesh, teasing, setting her ablaze. She twisted and bucked as fingers reached wetness and invaded in a slow, rhythmic movement.

"When you come awake, you really come awake, don't you?" she murmured, fighting the all-consuming sensation that threatened to sweep her over the edge before he had joined her.

"Don't fight me," he whispered back, the strokes more intense, deeper, more demanding.

She let go then, let the flood of feeling wash over her, through her. Then, just when she thought she would spin free, the touches slowed, taunted. Wild now with need, she pleaded silently, gazing into eyes darkened with passion.

"You want me?" he asked in that husky, low-down, sneaky tone that conjured images of the back-seat scrambling of adolescence, the hunger to try everything.

She wanted to say no, wanted to say she didn't need anyone, ever, but it would have been a lie. Right now, this instant, she couldn't bear the thought of one more second without him inside her, without that full, throbbing sense of completion.

Breathless, she rose instinctively toward him, hips lifting off the bed as she admitted between gasps, "I...want...you."

Satisfaction broke over his face as he joined her then with one powerful thrust. Even then, even when she felt she would explode with sensation—skin sensitive, fire in her veins—he took his time. He led her to the edge and back again and again, each time a little higher, the ride a little wilder until at last she felt the sweet waves of a shuddering climax consume first her and then him.

It was a long time before either of them spoke, before either of them could move. Kate was content to be held in his arms, her body still joined with his in the most intimate way possible. As long as they were together like this, she wouldn't have to decide whether to go or stay.

It was David who moved eventually, brushing a kiss on her bare shoulder as he left the bed and padded into the bathroom. She heard the shower go on and then, before she realized he'd returned, he had scooped her once again into his arms.

In the steamy bathroom she regarded the shower skeptically. "I'm not sure I trust you where water's concerned. Maybe I'd better test this myself before I plunge in."

He grinned. "It's warm. I promise," he said, standing her on her feet at the edge of the huge sunken tub. He grabbed a towel and headed for the door. "You go ahead. I'll pull on my suit and go for another swim."

Startled and disappointed that he wouldn't be joining her, she warned herself not to show it. "How can you possibly have that much energy to spare?" she said, too cheerfully. "I'm drained."

"I'm not sure I do. If you hear me yell, I trust you'll come save me."

She gave him a considering look, then forced a grin. "Yeah, I suppose I would."

He chuckled and left her then. Uneasy and unable to explain exactly why, Kate didn't linger under the steamy spray, even though it felt wonderful. Something inside nagged that she and David ought to be talking about what had happened, not suddenly ignoring it. She sensed that his retreat in that bed a few minutes earlier had been more than just physical. There had been something in his eyes, a shadow of regret perhaps, that reminded her that she should have heeded all those warnings to stay away. She toweled herself dry, then remembered that her clothes were still in the pool house.

Wrapped in the oversize towel, she started to walk back into the bedroom. Then she saw David standing beside the bed, head bent, shoulders slumped. A man in real torment. At first she wanted to run to him, but then she realized what had captured his attention so completely. He was holding a silver-framed picture in his hands. She'd noticed it herself earlier on the bedside table. It was his wedding picture.

She could feel the sting of tears in her eyes as she imagined the agony of regrets churning through him now. Reminded that the past few hours had been only an interlude, she felt her heart ache far more than it should have, given all the stern lectures she'd given herself lately. Obviously, intellectually knowing something was a far cry from the gut-wrenching pain of experiencing it emotionally.

It shouldn't have mattered. She had never wanted anything from any man, least of all this one. Clutching the towel together as she debated what to do, she finally admitted to herself that she had lied.

It was a lie that was going to cost her dearly.

Chapter Thirteen

If nothing else over recent weeks, Kate had learned a couple of valuable lessons. Nothing ever got solved by shoving it into a closet and ignoring it. Her own problems with her family, and Davey's problems with his father, were proof of that. The wounds had festered far longer than they'd needed to.

With that in mind, she crossed the bedroom until she was standing next to David. Careful not to brush against him, she said quietly, "She was very beautiful."

A sigh shuddered through him. Without turning to look at her, he said, "Yes. She was." He opened the drawer of the nightstand beside the bed and started to put the picture inside.

Pushing her own feelings firmly aside, Kate stayed his hand. "Don't."

His gaze, dark with anguish, clashed with hers. "It's time to let go of the past. Isn't that what you've been telling me for weeks now?" he said angrily, slamming the drawer closed, the picture inside.

"Yes," she said evenly, opening the drawer and taking it back out. She placed it carefully in its former spot on the nightstand. "There's a difference between moving on with your life and locking the past away as if it had never happened. What message would it send to Davey if he saw that his mother's pictures had all been shoved away out of sight? He's already afraid to mention her for fear of upsetting you."

For the space of a heartbeat, he looked taken aback. Then, if anything, his eyes flashed even more stubbornly. "Surely one of those pop psychology books at your house has a chapter on grief," he said sarcastically. "Perhaps you should look it over. I suspect it says that everyone handles grief in his or her own way."

Kate tried not to lose her temper, but he was so damned bullheaded and irritating. "That's true," she shot back. "But you're not *handling* it at all."

She thought for an instant he might lash back at her, hoped for it, in fact.

Instead, he simply said coldly, "What would you know about having your life shattered? You're always in control, always so certain of what you should be doing, what everyone should be doing. I'm sure you refuse to allow any little ups and downs."

Kate winced at the unflattering image. All too recently, however, his description would have been on the money. After her breakup with Ryan she had sought control, prided herself on it. But that hadn't always been the case, and she had paid heavily for that mistake, just as it appeared likely she would pay again for having fallen in love with a man who wasn't ready to give himself to anyone.

"You're wrong," she said. "You see, a long time ago I fell in love with a man I was sure was the man of my dreams. We were in law school together, but he dropped out, decided that there were other ways he could help the poor and downtrodden. I thought it was the most idealistic decision he could have made. I was very proud of him."

She watched David for a reaction. His expression was stony, his gaze directed at the floor. She plunged on anyway, hoping something about the rarely told story would get through to him.

"It didn't stop me from finishing school, though. He thought I would join in his fight, but I didn't. I had always wanted to go into a big law firm. I had wanted to be a powerful divorce lawyer, not because I wanted the money or the fame, but because I wanted to be there for women who gave everything to a marriage and then, it seemed to me, were always getting taken when it came time for a settlement."

She smiled ruefully as she thought about what had happened after that. "We lived together. I volunteered with some of his causes at first, but then my own career took off, and I had less and less time. He took it personally, accused me of selling out. Finally he told me he was leaving. I guess by then I wasn't all that surprised, but that didn't stop it from hurting."

Now at last David was watching her intently. "There's more, isn't there? What happened then?"

"A few days later, while I was still mourning our lost dreams, I received some legal papers. He was filing for palimony. He wanted a cut of everything I'd earned. He figured it was his due for letting his career take a back seat to mine."

The disgust was evident in David's expression. "How the hell would he figure that?"

"It's amazing how facts can get twisted to suit someone's purposes," she said with a shrug.

"Did you give him what he wanted?"

"I wanted to rip his heart out. I wanted to drag him through the entire legal system and show the world what a lousy creep he was. I was persuaded it wasn't in my own best interests. We settled out of court. Pragmatically I know it's what I had to do to avoid a scandal that could have hurt my career, but it's a decision I still regret."

She met his gaze. "I'm sure you're wondering what this has to do with you and Alicia, but I am trying to make a point. What happened with Ryan made me angry and bitter. Ironically, it probably made me an even better divorce lawyer. It gave me my go-for-the-jugular edge. At any rate, I allowed it to color every choice I've made—or not made—about relationships. In other words, I stopped living, and for all the wrong reasons.''

She reached up and touched his cheek. ''You have happier memories. You know how wonderful love can be. That won't change if you move on with your life. It won't be a betrayal of Alicia. If anything, it will be the opposite, a testament that what you shared lives on in you.''

His expression instantly hardened, deliberately shutting her out. ''I really don't want to discuss Alicia,'' he said adamantly. ''I'm going for a swim.''

He walked off and left her staring after him. Kate saw then that for all of their closeness that day, for all of the physical intimacy, one very real barrier stood between them. Alicia.

Until David could deal with his grief, until he could bring his memories into the open and discuss her with Davey or Kate or anyone else, a part of him would remain locked away and unreachable. It wouldn't matter what he believed about having moved on.

If she tried to force David to discuss Alicia with her, he could easily call her motives into question. Urging him to have those same conversations with Davey, however, was another matter altogether. Davey needed to talk about his mother, he needed to remember those times before she got sick and he needed to share his grief not with Kate, not with strangers, but with his father.

And no matter the cost to her, she was going to see that it happened. Bringing Alicia's name into the open so the healing could begin would be her final gift to the two of them.

From a chair in the shade beside the pool, his head throbbing, David watched Kate slip from the bedroom to the pool house wrapped only in a towel. Even after making love to her twice already this morning, he wanted her again. His body, primed by recent reality rather than distant memories, responded like an adolescent's, with hard, urgent need.

Unfortunately, given his behavior not ten minutes earlier, effectively telling her to mind her own business, he doubted she was going to be too anxious to accommodate this sudden need he had to hold her in his arms again.

When Kate emerged from the pool house, he fully expected her to mumble a polite goodbye and take off. Instead, she strolled over as if nothing, *nothing,* had gone on between them. She poured herself a glass of orange juice and sat down opposite him as if she'd just dropped in to chat about the weather. Puzzled, he waited for the verbal knife to be unsheathed and aimed at his belly. He watched her uneasily.

"Expecting Davey soon?" she asked.

"Any minute now."

"Good."

"You going to stick around?"

"If you don't mind."

He shook his head. "I don't mind." What he minded was this sudden, cool inanity, but he couldn't think of a blasted way to end it. Actually, he could think of one way. He could finish the conversation she had tried to start inside. Given that alternative, he opted for silence and watched as Kate slipped farther and farther away, lost in her own thoughts.

He glanced up and saw Mrs. Larsen bustling toward them. If she had any clue about what he and Kate had been up to, it didn't show in her stoic expression.

"I thought I'd clean up these dishes if you're finished," she said. "Need to get things done around here if Davey's going to have those boys over tonight."

He glanced at Kate. "I don't need anything else. How about you?"

"Nope," she said, giving Mrs. Larsen a smile. "Thank you, though. It was a lovely breakfast."

The housekeeper nodded. "You staying for lunch?"

"I would like to see Davey," Kate said, glancing at David.

Which caught him between a rock and a hard place. He wanted her out of here so he could get his equilibrium back, maybe even figure out what the hell she was up to now. At the same time he wanted her to stay, so these thrilling new off-balance sensations would last. "By all means, stay," he said. "Davey would be furious if I let you get away before he sees you."

If Mrs. Larsen sensed the undercurrents, she ignored them. "I'll be fixing something around one o'clock, if that's okay."

"Something simple," David said. "I know you're baking all those cookies for tonight."

"Yes, sir," she said and lumbered off with the tray of breakfast dishes.

"So, what's happening tonight?" Kate inquired.

"Davey's having a sleepover. Eight of his friends are coming. I've given Mrs. Larsen the night off. Otherwise, I'm afraid she'd quit."

Kate's expression turned wistful. "I think it sounds like fun."

David regarded her skeptically. "Fun?"

"Sure. Ghost stories. Games. Lots of cookies."

"Don't forget the pizza."

"Pizza and cookies," she said, nodding approvingly. "Every kid's dream menu."

"You know," he said slyly, "if you play your cards right, you could wind up as a chaperon."

Instead of backing down instantly as he'd anticipated, she hesitated. Then, slowly, she beamed, as if the whole idea genuinely appealed to her. "You wouldn't mind?"

"Mind?" he said, refusing to examine the consequences of having this woman in his home overnight...in a guest room. "I'd welcome the prospect of adult conversation."

"Not from me. I intend to tell ghost stories, too." She looked uncertain. "Do you think Davey will object?"

"To your being here or to your sitting in on the ghost stories?"

"Either one."

"I think he'll be ecstatic to have you around. As for the ghost stories, it depends on whether you know any really scary ones."

"I think that between now and tonight, I ought to be able to dream up one that'll have them all hiding under the beds. What about you?"

"Forget the ghost stories. I was thinking of spending the entire evening under the bed with earplugs."

"No. No. No," she said, her eyes unexpectedly alight with laughter. "You have to get into the spirit of this."

"Just how many sleepovers have you hosted in your time?"

"Only one, for my youngest niece. It was for her thirteenth birthday. It wasn't any fun," she said with obvious disgust. "All they wanted to do was practice using makeup and styling each other's hair."

Startled by her genuine indignation, David suddenly found himself laughing with her, letting the tension finally ease away. "Oh, Kate, you really are something."

"I trust you'll remember that the next time I irritate you," she said.

"Do you intend to irritate me often?"

For an instant, she looked nonplussed, a little sad. "No." She stood up suddenly. "If I'm going to spend the night, I'd better go home and change and pick up a few odds and ends."

"I thought you were staying for lunch."

"I'll try to get back, but if I don't make it, tell Davey I'll be here tonight."

Suddenly David didn't want to be left alone with his thoughts. "Why don't I drive you? I can pick up the soft drinks for tonight."

She hesitated, then nodded finally. "Sure."

On the way through the house, he stopped to tell Mrs. Larsen they were going out. "Anything else you think we need for tonight?" he asked her.

"Extra toothbrushes," the housekeeper suggested. "Kids never remember their toothbrushes."

The instant they were outside, Kate met his gaze. "Don't you dare buy extra toothbrushes. Half the fun of staying out overnight is not having to do all those things your parents are always insisting you do. Nobody's teeth will rot between tonight and when they go home tomorrow."

He grinned back at her. "Does that mean if you and I stay out overnight one of these days, you'll want to break all kinds of rules?"

"Oh, I think we've already broken about as many rules as we're going to," she said quietly.

Something in her voice stunned David into silence. She sounded as if she'd looked into the future and no longer saw them together. The very thought of losing her sent a chill through him.

The din from the family room echoed through the entire house. Kate slapped a throw pillow to either ear and went in search of David.

"Whose idea was this?" she demanded loudly when she found him.

"What?" he shouted back.

His voice barely topped the sound of some musical group that relied heavily on bass. Kate could feel the whole house vibrating. She stepped close and plucked the earplug from his ear.

"I asked whose idea this was."

"Yours, I think," he said. "You wanted my son and me to get closer. I think you wanted to be nearby to observe the bonding."

"If this is bonding, it's not all it's cracked up to be," she grumbled. "They don't even know we're here."

"I'm sorry about the ghost stories," he said sympathetically. "I know you were really counting on telling them."

Kate grimaced. When she had suggested telling ghost stories, nine boys had stared at her uncomprehendingly. Davey had informed her privately in an undertone that that was baby stuff. "I guess I caught them two or three years too late."

"You could tell me one," David suggested. "Or I could tell you about the next Stephen King picture. It's a guaranteed spine tingler."

Kate shrugged. "It wouldn't be the same. Is there any pizza left?"

"Are you kidding? That went ten minutes after the delivery man dropped it off. Too bad they don't give you a discount if you can eat it faster than they can deliver it." He held out a hand. "Come with me, though. Mrs. Larsen left a secret stash of roast beef sandwiches for us."

Kate sighed. "Wonderful."

He poured them both mineral water and put the plate of sandwiches on the kitchen table. Kate watched the fleeting look of dismay that crossed his face and wondered if he was thinking again that this was something he should have been sharing with Alicia. When he sat down across from her, though, his gaze was free of whatever had been troubling him.

She, however, couldn't shake that bleak mood so easily. It reminded her once more that the memory of tonight was all she would have left soon. She had to force David and Davey to face their grief and when she did, David wouldn't thank her for it. Maybe someday, but certainly not now. And yet she had no choice. David would be living only half a life as long as a part of himself remained buried with Alicia.

So she would have this one night of feeling as if they were a family and in the morning she would do what had to be done and then she would move on and try to put her own life in order. Alone, as usual. She had to blink hard against the sting of tears.

She looked at David and forced a smile. "Davey's having the time of his life," Kate said, determined to put on a brave front so that he would never know how much it hurt her to know that even when they were most intimate Alicia had come between them, would always be there between David and any woman, unless she found a way to free him. "Is this the first time he's ever had a sleepover?"

"Yeah. I must say I wasn't sure what to expect," he confessed. "When I was a kid, I occasionally had a friend over, but never a whole gang like this."

"But I imagine living in a college dorm is a similar experience," Kate said.

"Maybe. I didn't live in a dormitory. I lived at home."

"Me, too," Kate said wistfully. "I wanted to go to a really good law school and that meant going to one within commuting distance. I couldn't have afforded to go away to one of the Ivy League schools."

"Did you feel you missed out on a lot by living off campus?" David asked.

She nodded. "The social things, yes. I don't suppose it really mattered, though. I met Ryan my sophomore year, and that was that."

"Do you suppose you fell into a pattern with him because you didn't have an opportunity to meet a lot of other students socially?"

Kate considered the question thoughtfully. "You may be right. We met in the library. Just a couple of studious loners, I guess."

"And here you are with me, another loner."

"A loner, maybe," she said. "But not a misfit. I think that was Ryan's problem. He *prided* himself on being a social outcast. Trying to live a normal life with someone like that creates a real strain. I think I was beginning to resent that even before he walked out."

"Maybe he anticipated that you were getting ready to cut him loose and wanted to beat you to it. The palimony business was his way of making you notice he was going."

"A last bid for attention?" she said, surprised by his perceptiveness. "Could have been, I suppose." She met David's gaze. "It doesn't seem to matter anymore."

It was ironic, she supposed, that this had been his gift to her. After all this time she had finally left the past behind. She was no longer afraid to love again.

And now she had to let go of the man who'd made that happen.

Kate awoke in the guest room the next morning with sunlight streaming through a window and a ten-year-old asleep beside her. As soon as she rolled over, Davey's eyes blinked wide and a grin spread across his face.

"Hi, Kate."

"Hey, sleepyhead, what're you doing in here?"

"I came in to check on you after everybody left this morning. You were still asleep. I guess I was pretty sleepy, too, so I lay down." He regarded her uncertainly. "Was that okay?"

"Absolutely," she said, thinking of how wonderful it felt to have this child trust her so completely, to have him take her into his heart the way he had. This was yet another of those moments she would hold close through the years. A child's love was so simple and straightforward. It was only between grown-ups that the emotion got complicated.

Suddenly the rest of Davey's explanation struck her. "You said everyone's gone?"

"Yeah, a while ago."

"What time is it?" she asked, reaching for her watch.

"Probably eleven o'clock," Davey guessed.

"Closer to noon," Kate said with a groan. She hadn't slept this late in years. "Is your dad up?"

"I don't think so. He looked pretty beat when he finally went to bed."

"Indeed he did," Kate agreed, thinking of his half-asleep kiss at the guest room door sometime after four this morning. He'd missed her lips. The kiss had landed in the vicinity of her nose. "Well, since Mrs. Larsen isn't here, suppose you and I go clean up and fix breakfast."

"The guys helped to clean up," Davey said, bounding out of bed. He frowned. "I think we probably need to vacuum, though. Mrs. Larsen will have a heart attack if she finds popcorn stuck under all the cushions."

"To say nothing of pepperoni and cookie crumbs."

He grinned. "Yeah, that, too."

Actually, the boys had at least put the furniture back into upright positions and replaced most of the cushions. They'd even lugged the trash into the kitchen. Three garbage bags full.

"Not so bad," Kate observed, bending down to retrieve the green pepper she'd almost squished into the carpet. "Where's the vacuum?"

"I'll get it," Davey said, dashing off and returning with it a few minutes later.

"Okay, I'll run this, if you'll get a rag and dust. You go first so that all the crumbs are on the floor when I start."

While Davey got the cleanup started, she made a pot of coffee and fought against the feelings of belonging that kept sneaking up on her. It was almost impossible to resist the magical allure of believing that this was her house, that Davey was her child and that the man still asleep upstairs was hers, as well.

But that couldn't be, she reminded herself. Not until the past was well and truly buried. And after she said what she had to say this morning to make that happen, David might never forgive her.

She refused to let anticipation of the confrontation to come ruin these last precious moments, though. She was humming as she ran the vacuum from room to room with Davey darting ahead of her, turning it into a game, making her laugh.

Suddenly she looked up and spotted David standing in an archway, his jeans riding low on his hips, his chambray shirt hanging loose. His cheeks were stubbled with the beginnings of a beard. His hair was mussed. It was a sexy, masculine look that had her whole body crying to march back into his room and tumble into bed with him.

"Good Lord, what's all this racket?" he murmured in a husky, sleepy voice that teased her senses.

"It's the morning after," she told him.

"After what?" he grumbled. "Did somebody set off a bomb in here? You've been making that infernal racket for hours now."

"Just trying to live up to Mrs. Larsen's high standards," she said, pushing the vacuum into one last corner. She beamed at him as she switched it off. "All done now."

"Thank God."

"You don't do well in the morning, do you?"

"I do wonderfully well when morning comes after a night of sleep. This morning came after sleep deprivation that could have been used to elicit military secrets from the enemy."

"Well, pull yourself together, buddy. I am about to make some of my world-famous pancakes."

"World famous, huh?"

"They would be, if this weren't a secret recipe. Now move it."

He mumbled something about twisted personalities as he stumbled back toward the master suite. Davey peeked around a doorway. He grinned. "He's always cranky before he has his coffee."

"Then by all means take him some coffee," she suggested. "I just made a fresh pot."

While Davey did that, Kate fixed breakfast. She found silverware and napkins and, when Davey returned, sent them outside with him. "Fork on the left, knife and spoon on the right," she reminded him as he dashed off.

David reappeared just as she was about to pour the pancake batter onto the sizzling hot griddle. He smelled of soap and some sort of minty mouthwash. No after-shave. Just the pure masculine scent of a man who'd freshly showered. She decided that all those manufacturers of sexy shaving lotions were wasting their time. There was nothing more alluring than this.

He propped himself against the counter and observed her in a way that was thoroughly disconcerting. "Don't mind me," he said when she stood there with a spoon in one hand, poised over the bowl of batter.

That was like asking the tides to ignore the moon, she thought grumpily, but she ladled the batter onto the griddle and listened to the satisfying sizzle. "If you're going to stick around in here, grab that plate," she said, flipping the golden pancakes over and fighting an unexpected urge to cry. How was she going to walk away from this? The temptation to try to hold on tight, to compromise and accept just a small part of David's heart, was almost too great.

When David had the plate in hand, she scooped up the first batch of pancakes. He took them and started for the door.

"Hey, where do you think you're going?"

"I've got mine. I'm going to eat."

"Oh, no, you don't. Come back here. That plate's for all of them."

"But these'll get cold."

"Not if I keep adding warm ones on top. Now stand still. Here's another batch."

She flipped at least a dozen onto the plate before she shooed him out of the kitchen. "Share those with your son."

He leaned down and dropped a kiss on the end of her nose. "You look cute all dusted with flour."

Kate groaned and rubbed at the offending flour as he walked out the door. She turned one last batch of pancakes onto another plate and followed.

All during breakfast, she couldn't keep her glance from straying first to David, then to the pool, and then to the master bedroom just beyond. He seemed to be studiously avoiding exactly the same kind of survey. Occasionally their gazes caught and Kate felt an embarrassed flush creep over her.

Unfortunately, she couldn't help thinking about the way yesterday morning had ended, as well. She glanced at Davey and then at his father. Drawing in a deep breath, she made a decision. Putting this off wouldn't solve anything. It might give her a few more memories, but the agony of leaving would be just as inevitable.

"Davey, I'll bet your mom would have liked seeing you with all your friends last night," she said casually.

Davey's eyes widened, and his gaze darted to his father. He mumbled something under his breath.

Kate determinedly pressed on. "David, don't you think Alicia would have liked having all the kids stay over?"

He glared at her. "What the hell are you trying to do?" he muttered finally. He shoved his chair back as if he was about to take off.

"I'm trying to have a perfectly normal conversation."

"Not now," David insisted, scowling at her furiously.

"Yes, now," she retorted stubbornly. "Davey, what's the one thing you remember most about your mom?"

"She was..." he began and then his voice broke off as he stared guiltily at his father.

Kate kept her gaze pinned on David, willing him to respond. Finally he swallowed hard.

"She was what, son?" he said in a voice that was barely above a whisper.

"She smelled like flowers and she was pretty and fun," he said softly. Tears welled up in his eyes.

"Yes, she was," David replied, his own face ashen.

Davey was staring at the table. "I miss her, Dad. I'm sorry but I really miss her."

Tears spilled down Kate's cheeks as she waited. Her hands were clenched into fists in her lap. Please, she murmured silently. Please.

Finally, his voice choked and gruff, David said, "I miss her, too, son."

Davey's sobs broke then, and he scrambled into his father's arms. David's gaze clashed with hers, his expression filled with something very close to loathing. Then he murmured something to Davey and refused to look at her at all.

Numb with her own pain, Kate left them like that, grabbing her bag from inside the guest room and hurrying to her car. She waited until she was down the hill before she pulled to the curb and allowed her own tears to fall freely.

Chapter Fourteen

The ache in Kate's heart wouldn't go away. Time and again she told herself that she'd done what she had to do. She had pushed David and Davey into talking about Alicia. Surely their relationship was mending more rapidly now. And that, after all, was the only reason she'd involved herself in their lives in the first place.

At least, that was how it had started. Somewhere along the way she had fallen in love. She had taken father and son into her heart, allowed them to become woven into the fabric of her life. No matter how frequently she told herself that letting go was for the best, it didn't stop the hurt. She'd expected David not to forgive her, but his absence was painful just the same, even worse than she'd anticipated.

She was going through the motions of living, consuming raspberry tea by the potful as if that could soothe the pain. She was going into court, presenting strong cases for her clients. She was consoling others still struggling with the decision of whether to fight for a marriage or leave. Far more often than she might have only weeks ago, she encouraged them to fight. To ward off the memories, she kept her calendar booked from early morning until late at night.

Despite the crammed days, her life was emptier than ever. For the first time in years, she found herself reevaluating her own needs and expectations based on a different set of priorities. It was a process she'd begun just before meeting David. He had only served to magnify the changes that were needed if she was ever to find real happiness. In pushing him toward the one thing that really mattered, bottom line, she had discovered it for herself, as well.

As she sat in her office at the end of the day, lost in thought, she tried to put a positive spin on the muddle her life seemed to be in. Taking stock was good. She owed David Winthrop a debt of gratitude for forcing her to engage in some heavy-duty soul-searching.

Unfortunately, she didn't much like what she saw. All the success suddenly seemed shallow without someone with whom to share it. She knew her mother was proud, knew that Ellen on occasion even envied her career. Her peers respected her. Her clients thought she walked on water. None of it seemed to matter. No, that wasn't quite right. It didn't seem to matter as much. She wanted the balance of a personal life, someone like David with whom she could share her problems and her successes, someone who would be there to console her or rejoice with her.

Stop hedging, she lectured herself in disgust. She wanted to share her life with David Winthrop, not just someone like him. She wanted him to show her the way to feel so deeply that not even death could break the bond.

Late on Friday night, Kate stared at the pile of work on her desk and contemplated yet another lonely, work-filled weekend. This was the path she'd chosen, she reminded herself sternly as she shoved papers helter-skelter into her briefcase.

"It's going to take you half the night to sort those out," a low, husky voice commented from the doorway.

Kate's gaze shot up. Pleasure seemed to vibrate through her. "David!"

He regarded her somberly. "Hello, Kate."

She hoped he couldn't hear the sudden thundering of her heart, wished she weren't quite so aware of it herself. As she hungrily searched his face, she noted the tiredness in his eyes, the lines in his forehead. For a man whose life should have been back on an even keel, he looked miserable. Nor was there any hint of anger. That puzzled her.

"What brings you by?" she asked, not allowing herself to hope.

"We need to talk."

She shook her head, denying the need. "I don't think so."

"Don't you even want to know how Davey and I are getting along?"

"Of course, but . . ."

"Then have dinner with me."

She couldn't go through this again, couldn't get so close to him and to Davey only to have Alicia come between them again. She snatched at the first, most obvious excuse. "I have plans."

He shook his head. "No, you don't. I checked with Zelda."

"She doesn't keep track of my personal calendar."

He smiled ruefully. "Kate, you don't have a personal calendar. Now stopping arguing and let's get out of here. I made a reservation."

Her chin rose stubbornly. "You should have called first."

"I did."

"You didn't talk to me."

"No, I didn't. I figured you'd already written the final farewell scene when you walked out of my house a couple of weeks ago. You're too obstinate to admit that it could have a very different ending."

Her gaze challenged his. "David, why are you doing this?"

"Because *I* don't think things are over between us. I think they're just beginning."

"You're wrong," she said, fiercely trying to protect herself from the anguish of parting all over again. Pride and determination had gotten her away from his house the first time. She wasn't sure either was strong enough to be tested again.

"Are you saying you don't . . . ?" He hesitated over the choice of words, his gaze searching hers. "Are you saying that you don't care for me? Do you want me to believe that the way you've involved yourself with Davey and with me was the same way you'd treat any other case?"

Kate couldn't bring herself to lie. But she did hedge. "Of course you weren't just another case. I do care for you and for Davey. I always will. But that's where it ends."

"Why?"

Couldn't he see that she wouldn't settle for less than what he'd shared with Alicia? "Caring is not the same as love. We both deserve bells and whistles."

He chuckled and lifted his gaze heavenward in disbelief. "I guess you weren't in that bed with me a few weeks back, then," he observed wryly. "I've heard magnificent, centuries-old church bells that chimed with less intensity."

"You're just grateful because I helped with Davey."

"Kate, what I feel is a hell of a lot more powerful than gratitude." He pinned her with his gaze. "I am very close to wanting to strip those damned, conservative clothes off you, so I can take you right on top of your desk just to prove how wrong you are."

Blood roared in Kate's ears, and fiery anticipation danced through her. "That's just sex," she said dismissively, but her voice was oddly breathless.

David grinned. "Yes, it is. Hot, steamy, hungry sex. We do it damned well, Kate." He stepped closer and cupped her chin, his gaze locked with hers. "Don't we?"

Her breath snagged. She closed her eyes, trying to block out the images he'd aroused. She couldn't. They filled her head. They filled her heart. Memories, she reminded herself firmly. They were just memories. They would fade in time.

But this was now, and David was flesh-and-blood real. His sly, potent virility was casting a spell over her this instant. Kate wanted to believe, but she didn't dare. Believing led to heartache, pain even worse than the agony she was feeling at this moment. Her gift to him was the freedom to move on. Nothing more.

"Please," she pleaded. "Don't try to make this into something it isn't. You've just gotten used to having me around the last few weeks. You don't need me. Not really."

"Yes, I do," he said softly. "Davey and I both need you and I will prove that if it takes me forever to do it."

Then with a faint sigh, he leaned down and touched his lips to hers. The gentleness of that touch shook her far more than the persuasive command of which she knew he was capable. The tenderness shattered resolve and chased away rational thought. She could almost believe then that he'd meant what he said. He needed her. It was a start, but no matter how hard she tried to believe it was enough, she knew that she wanted more. She wanted his love.

                              *   *   *

"Why won't you take the man's calls?" Zelda demanded days later. "He's beginning to drive me crazy."

"I pay you to deal with persistent, unwanted callers."

"Unwanted? I don't think so," she said smugly.

"Zelda, if you are not very careful, I will introduce you to my new stepfather and tell him I'm worried about the state of your love life," Kate warned.

Zelda's laughter bounced off the walls. "Is that supposed to scare me?"

Kate frowned. "It terrifies me." In fact, she was flat-out horrified that Brandon would somehow learn that she was no longer seeing David Winthrop and would set out to do something about it.

"I wouldn't mind having someone rich and successful and intelligent look around for the right guy for me," Zelda said dreamily. "Brandon Halloran probably travels in much more interesting circles than I do." She regarded Kate with a disapproving look. "You realize that you're avoiding the real problem here."

"Oh? What problem is that?"

"You're scared," she accused. "Knee-shaking, pain-in-the-gut scared."

"Maybe so," Kate conceded with a sigh. "Maybe so."

Not five minutes later, Zelda buzzed. "Call on line one."

"Who is it?" she asked, but she was talking to herself. Filled with trepidation, she stared at the flashing light on her phone. Finally, because she absolutely refused to be ruled by cowardice, she gingerly picked up the receiver. "Hello."

"Hi, Kate, it's me," Davey said.

She breathed a faint sigh of relief. "Well, hi, yourself. How're you doing?"

"I'm okay," he said, and for once Kate believed him. She could hear the change in his voice. "I called to invite you to a ball game."

"Me?" she asked, inexplicably pleased. This was the first time she'd talked to her client since that day at the house. She thought he'd probably become so caught up in reestablishing his relationship with his dad that he'd forgotten all about her.

"Yeah. And guess what? I'm going to play quarterback."

"Davey, that's wonderful." At least, she thought it was. He certainly sounded as if it was.

"Will you come? I haven't seen you for a really long time."

"I'm sorry. I've been really busy, but I've missed you a lot. Now about the game, shouldn't you be asking your dad?"

"Oh, he's already promised to come, but I want you, too."

She couldn't go. It would hurt too much. But when she hesitated, he added, "All the other kids will have their moms there."

Kate felt as if the floor had dropped out from under her. "Oh, Davey," she whispered, her voice choked. How could she resist a plea like that, especially when it appealed to the yearning deep inside her, as well?

"Okay, I'll come," she said finally, after considering and rejecting every single logical reservation she had about going.

"Thanks, Kate. You're the greatest."

"Where and when?"

He gave her directions to the field. "It's six o'clock tonight."

Tonight? Kate thought, suddenly panicked. How could she slam all her defenses into place that quickly?

"You won't be late, will you?" Davey asked worriedly.

"Not if I can help it," she promised.

As soon as she'd hung up, however, she regretted making the commitment. How was she going to get through an entire evening pretending that she was no more than a casual acquaintance, when Davey seemed hell-bent on having her fill in as his mother?

"You going to that game?" Zelda inquired from the doorway.

Kate's gaze shot up. "What do you know about that?"

"A little birdie told me," her secretary announced smugly.

"A little birdie or a grown-up birdie?" Kate inquired suspiciously.

"Sorry. Confidential," Zelda retorted. "Enjoy yourself. You'd better get going if you plan to change and be there by six."

"Don't I have an appointment at five?"

"Postponed until tomorrow."

Kate sighed. She should have guessed. "Any other plots afoot that I should know about?"

Zelda shook her head. "Nope. This is my last nudge. From now on you're on your own."

"Thank God," Kate said fervently. Ironically, though, the reassurance didn't bring nearly as much comfort as it should have.

There were at least a hundred parents in the bleachers when Kate arrived. Her gaze zeroed in on David as easily as if he'd been wearing neon. He lounged at the end of a row, his gaze focused first on the field, then shifting to search the parking lot. The sun shot his hair with gold.

As soon as she stepped out of her car, a smile spread across his face. That slow, lazy smile should have been outlawed in polite society. To her regret, it warmed her down to her toes.

"Hi," he said when she neared the stands. "I wasn't sure you'd come."

"Davey told you I'd be here?"

"Actually, I suggested he call." At her look of dismay over the low-down, sneaky tactics, he added quickly, "It didn't take any persuasion, Kate."

He held out a hand and helped her up. To Kate's dismay—and relief—he didn't let go, not until her hand had been warmed by the contact, not until half the people around them had taken note of the possessive gesture.

"Has the game started yet?" she asked, unable to keep the shaky note from her voice.

"They've run one series of plays. The other team couldn't convert on third down. We have the ball."

"English, please," she demanded.

His eyes widened. "Kate, haven't you ever been to a football game before?"

She shook her head. "Afraid not."

"But you went to UCLA," he protested.

"I spent all my time in the library. I told you that."

"What about now? We have two professional teams in this area."

"And I have season tickets for both. I give them to clients."

"Dear Lord."

She frowned at him. "Davey said he's the quarterback. Is that good?"

David laughed. "It is if he completes his passes."

Kate tried to concentrate on the game after that. She wasn't always absolutely certain what was going on, but she took her cues from the fans and from the man seated beside her. He spent most of the game muttering advice under his breath. The advice was clearly meant for Davey.

"Why aren't you shouting at him like everyone else?"

"I won't put that kind of pressure on him. He's a kid. He should be enjoying the game. If he asks me later, I'll tell him what I thought he could improve, but I won't badger him while he's out there. He's doing the best he can."

He shook his head and glanced around them. "Listen to the way some of these parents carry on. It's a wonder their children sign up to play at all."

Kate listened to the shouts around them more closely and decided—totally objectively, of course—that David was quite possibly the best parent in the stands. But that was no real surprise. She'd always believed in the strength of his relationship with his son. She was glad that she'd come, if only to see that the bond between them had been fully restored.

With the score tied at ten, Davey went back on the field with less than a minute to play. Kate found herself on her feet, cheering as hard as anyone around her. She glanced up and caught David watching her and shrugged.

"I guess I got a little caught up in the spirit of things."

"Don't apologize. That's the idea," he said, just as Davey threw something that David described as a Hail Mary pass.

The boy it was meant for stumbled, then lunged into the air, arms outstretched. Kate's breath caught in her throat as she waited for that ball to come down. It seemed to linger on his fingertips for an eternity before he gathered it close and fell forward over the goal line.

The parents in the stands went wild, including Kate. She threw her arms around David. "Did you see that?

Did you see how Davey's pass went straight into that boy's arms? What a pass!"

"Give the receiver a little credit," David teased.

"Well, sure, but it was Davey who got the ball down there. The ball didn't even wobble. What an arm!" she said, echoing the praise she'd heard around her.

David's tolerant smile finally penetrated her exuberance.

"Sorry," she apologized.

"For what?" He touched her cheek with his fingertips. "Do you have any idea what it does to me to share this with you?"

Kate felt the salty sting of tears in her eyes and tried to look away, but he wouldn't let her.

"We were meant to be like this," he insisted. "You and me and Davey. We could be a real family, Kate."

A family. The words seemed to echo in her heart. Oh, how she wanted that. But she refused to allow herself to hope. Before she could utter a denial, Davey came racing toward them. He was caught up in his father's hug.

"You were terrific, son."

"Thanks, Dad. Did you see, Kate? That pass was the longest one I've ever thrown. Ever!"

She smiled at his excitement. "I'm really glad I was here to see it."

"I think a celebration is in order," David said, his gaze on Kate, pleading with her not to spoil things for Davey.

Because she wanted one last memory to tuck away with all the rest, she nodded slowly. "A celebration sounds terrific."

But Davey, it seemed, had his own plans for celebrating with his friends. David didn't seem nearly as surprised by that information as he might have been.

"I guess it's just you and me, then," he said, linking Kate's arm through his as Davey ran off to join his friends. "My place? We can raid the refrigerator."

He made it sound so incredibly casual and spontaneous that Kate couldn't find the words to refuse. "Sure," she said finally. "I'll follow you."

"Why not ride with me and I'll bring you back to your car later?"

Which would effectively strand her at his house until he had used every bit of persuasion at his disposal to convince her that they had a future, she thought. No, thanks! She smiled. "I think I'll drive."

He shrugged. "Whatever. I'll meet you there, then."

Kate followed him up the winding narrow road into Bel Air. By the time they reached the house, the lights of Los Angeles were spread out below as if stardust had been sprinkled on the valley floor. At the house David poured them each a glass of wine and led the way onto the terrace so they could take full advantage of the view. The awareness sizzling between them was almost palpable.

"I'm glad you came," David said quietly.

"I didn't want to disappoint Davey," she said.

"I'm not talking about the game, Kate," he said with a touch of impatience. "I'm talking about here. Did you not want to disappoint me, as well?"

She sighed. "I'm not exactly sure why I came. I should have known that sooner or later you'd force us back into the same conversation."

David slowly put his glass aside and with his gaze locked with hers, he took her glass and set it on the table. "No conversation, Kate."

Kate's heart thumped unsteadily as he pulled her into his arms. Damn it all to hell, she didn't even try to resist. She went willingly, yearning for the feel of his body pressed into hers, hungering for his lips to plunder hers. With a little cry that was part pleasure, part dismay, she opened her mouth to the invasion of his tongue. The fantasy world spread out below them seemed to reach up to draw them in.

This, Kate told herself, this was what she was giving up. She could feel David's heart thundering beneath her palm, the scratch of his faintly stubbled skin against her cheek, the hardness of his manhood pressed against her. Each sensation was distinct and separate. Each blended into a thrilling swirl of desire that swept through her and left her dazed with need.

Why couldn't she just accept this moment? Why couldn't she take whatever part of David's heart he had left to give and be satisfied?

Because she'd seen what he was capable of giving, she admitted finally. And she wanted it all, wanted the full power of his love and attention. She couldn't share it with a ghost.

"No," she said, far too late, when her body was crying out for satisfaction. "David, no."

His jaw clenched with anger, he stepped away. He picked up his glass, finished the wine in one gulp, then drank what was left of hers. Only then did he allow his gaze to clash with hers. Kate shuddered at the hot fury in his eyes.

"Why?" he bit out.

"I'm not in the mood."

"Dammit, I am not referring to sex. I'm talking about us."

"There is no us."

"Then I'll ask one more time, why?"

For Kate the answer was simple. One word. "Alicia."

He regarded her incredulously. "Kate, for God's sake, Alicia is dead."

"But you haven't stopped grieving for her. If I doubted that before, your reaction just now to the mention of her name was proof that it's the truth."

David shoved his hand through his hair and began to pace, leaving Kate to stand alone in the chill air, shivering. Finally, when he turned to face her again, his expression was anguished.

"No," he corrected softly. "It's not grief. It's a lot of things, Kate, but not grief."

Stunned by the note of despair in his voice, she stared at him incredulously. "But what, then?"

"Guilt. Anger, maybe."

"I don't understand."

"I was glad when she died, Kate," he said, looking heartbroken by the admission. "Glad! What kind of creature does that make me? What kind of father could I be when I wanted my son's mother to die? I wanted to see her suffering over with. I wanted desperately for things to get back to normal."

A sigh shuddered through him. "Only when she was gone did I see that they never would be normal again. And that made me angry, at her, at God, at myself. Every single time you attributed me with this noble passion, this gut-deep sorrow, I felt like a fraud."

She reached out to him, but he shook her off.

"No, let me finish. Don't get me wrong. I loved her. She was an intelligent, beautiful, gentle, lovely woman. But in the end, she wasn't even Alicia anymore, and I hated myself for feeling that way."

"Oh, David," Kate said, her voice catching. "I'm so sorry."

He regarded her with a wry expression. "So, you see, I'm not at all the man you thought I was."

"Yes," she said firmly, "you are. What do you think grief is? It is anger and pain and a sense of loss and maybe even some guilt all rolled into one shattering emotion. Do you think you are the only person ever to be glad to see an end to a loved one's suffering? Do you think you are the only man ever to feel anger and resentment at being left alone?"

She touched his cheek, and this time he didn't withdraw. "But you will work your way through those emotions in time. I can promise you that. Just by admitting the feelings to me tonight, I think you're already well on your way."

"Am I asking too much if I ask you to go through this with me? I need you, Kate."

Need, not love, she thought dismally. "I will always be your friend," she said, because it was all she could say without showing the depth of her vulnerability. "I'm going now, but we'll talk soon."

"What about dinner?"

She shrugged. "I think food is the last thing either of us has on our minds."

She stood on tiptoe then, and pressed a kiss to his cheek. As she turned and walked away, she wondered when or if she would ever share a kiss with him again.

Chapter Fifteen

The bed trembled as if it were being shaken by an ill-tempered giant, jarring Kate awake, her heart thundering in her chest.

An earthquake! A huge one, if the rolling motion of the room was any indication. Her equilibrium went off kilter, rendering her almost as nauseous as if she'd been on the deck of a boat caught in an ocean's swells.

When she could move, she raced for a doorway and braced herself against the building's terrifying sway that had light fixtures swinging back and forth from the ceiling. Outside she could see the frantic to-and-fro movement of light poles, heard the crackle and fiery pop of a transformer before the street was plunged into darkness.

All her life she had lived with the frightening threat of earthquakes, had accepted it as part of the price for living in LA. Earthquakes were among the few things in life absolutely beyond her control. She tried to be prepared and left it at that.

Over the years she had experienced scary tremors and mild aftershocks with minimal psychological scars. She knew this terrible creaking and rocking would end, but when it did, what would be left?

This one seemed to be going on longer than usual, its force more powerful than any she could recall from recent years. She knew it had to be centered far closer than the strong quakes that had hit the desert the previous summer, nearly a hundred miles away and still terrifying.

She heard the doors on her kitchen cabinets open and slam, open and slam, followed by the breaking of glass.

With her adrenaline pumping by the time the awesome quaking stopped, she found slippers, then inched her way carefully to the kitchen, where she kept earthquake supplies. She turned on a battery-powered light, then the battery-powered radio.

"A quake estimated to be at least seven point five or greater on the Richter scale has just shaken downtown Los Angeles. Reports from Cal State indicate the quake was centered in West Hollywood. Our studios on Sunset have cracks in the walls. Studio windows popped out. We can see from here that glass is out in some downtown office buildings. Several residents in the Beverly Hills and Bel Air area have called to report smelling gas. We have reporters heading into the area now and will be back with full details as they come in. Is this The Big One? Stay tuned.''

Bel Air, Kate thought, stricken. What about David and Davey? Were they okay? Their house sat high on a ridge overlooking a valley. Obviously it had weathered other quakes through the years, but if preliminary reports were talking about gas leaks and shattered glass, this could be far worse than anything it had ever sustained before. On top of the earthquake damage, gas leaks and downed power lines threatened fires.

She grabbed the phone and dialed. Only after she'd punched in the last number did she realize that there had never even been a dial tone. The line was out.

Frantic now, she grabbed a pair of jeans and a T-shirt and scrambled into them. She pulled on thick socks and sneakers, stopped for her kit of emergency supplies and bottled water and hurried into the building's hallway. It was dark as midnight.

No electricity, no elevator, she thought with dismay. She could make out the generator-powered red light above the doorway to the emergency stairwell and crept along the corridor, wasting precious time but unable to risk moving any faster. At last she reached the door and pushed it open. Using her flashlight to illuminate the stairs, she began making her way down twelve flights to the parking garage below. The trip seemed to take an eternity.

Eventually, though, she reached the car. As she sped up the exit ramp, she heard the distant, terrifying drone of sirens. Lots of sirens. She turned north on

Century Park East and then she saw the glow on the horizon. Not in the east where the sun would be breaking through, but northwest. In Bel Air. Where David and Davey were. Her stomach turned over as she considered the danger they were in.

Kate was halfway up the canyon road when she hit the first crevice, a crack sufficiently wide to jar the car. There were two more beyond that, each a little wider, a little more difficult to navigate. Ignoring tire damage and the threat hinted at by the increasing severity of those cracks, she drove on until she found her way blocked by a fallen tree.

All around her she saw families dazed by the quake, standing in their yards gazing at the aftermath. One whole wing of an estate had collapsed. A tree had tumbled on top of three cars in a single bricked driveway. And still, strong aftershocks kept the earth trembling.

Bullhorns warned of potential gas leaks and advised residents to avoid using electricity or candles until utility crews could get into the area. From every yard she could hear the hum of radio reports, updated every few minutes. The announcers, too, listed the hazards that followed earthquakes, reminding listeners of precautions to be taken.

Somewhere above her the warnings were already too late. She could see the glow of a fire, stronger now, feeding on the drought-stricken landscape. The acrid smell of smoke filled her nostrils.

Images of David and Davey crowded into her head as she pulled to the side of the road and determinedly set out on foot. Just as she rounded the next bend, a fireman blocked her way.

"Ma'am, you can't go up there."

Kate stared at him, uncomprehending. "But I have to," she said simply and kept walking.

He caught her arm and held her back. "It's not safe."

Her gaze clashed with his. "But David is there and his son. I have to find them."

The fireman, a young man with streaks of soot on his already weary face, regarded her sympathetically. "I'm sorry. I can't let you do that. Wait here. We're evacuating the people from up there now."

"But what if they're injured?" she said, her voice catching on a sob.

"We'll get them out, ma'am."

Defeated, Kate walked to the side of the road and sank down on the trunk of an upended tree. Tears cut streaks down her cheeks as she kept her gaze pinned to the road and the straggle of residents making their way down from higher ground.

They had to be all right, she told herself over and over. She couldn't lose them. Whether they were her real family or not, she loved them as if they were. An image of David swam before her eyes, a teasing I-told-you-so glint in his eyes. She choked back a sob. He would come to her eventually, if only to say those words, if only to taunt her for taking so blasted long to admit something he had accepted weeks ago.

Family, she thought as the smoke seemed to surround her. Dear Lord, she hadn't given a thought to her mother and Brandon or to Ellen and her family. Chances were good, given the preliminary estimate of the quake's epicenter, that they'd received no more than the same awakening jolt she had. Still, she had to check. She thought, belatedly, of her car phone.

Reluctant to leave where she was, she realized that she had no real choice anyway. The smoke was becoming more dense by the minute, and she could see by the expression on the fireman's face that at any second he was going to insist that she move farther out of the path of danger.

She trudged back down the winding road until she reached her car. She tried first to call David, but there was no answer at the house. Because he was already moving out of harm's way, she told herself firmly. Even though she wanted with all her heart to believe that, she couldn't help envisioning him pinned under a fallen beam or trapped on the far side of the fire.

Trembling with the agony of waiting, she dialed her mother's house. "Mom?" she said and then her voice broke.

"Kate, darling, are you okay? I've been calling and calling, but your damned phone isn't working."

"I'm sorry I didn't call sooner. As soon as it happened, I saw that there was a fire over in Bel Air."

"And you started worrying about David?" her mother guessed. "Is he okay?"

"I don't know," she said bleakly. "I can't get all the way up to the house. The fire's getting worse. It's driving me crazy. I don't like sitting on the sidelines and waiting this way. I want to do something."

"Charging to the rescue," her mother said, and Kate could practically see her smile. "Oh, Katie, darling, you can't save the world."

"Maybe not," she admitted. "But I've given it a damned good shot." She hesitated. "Mom?"

"Yes, darling?"

"I think I'm ready to think about saving myself."

"Is that your way of saying you've fallen in love with David Winthrop?"

Kate laughed. "Yes, I guess it is." It was such an overwhelming relief to be able to speak the words aloud. "I love David Winthrop."

Suddenly she heard someone pounding on the window of the car and looked up to see David, sooty and rumpled, but very much alive. He was grinning at her and she knew that he'd heard, but it didn't seem to matter anymore that she'd put her heart on the line.

"He's here," Kate shouted, jubilant. "Mom, I'll talk to you later, all right?" Then, almost as an afterthought, she said, "You are okay, aren't you? And Ellen?"

"Everyone is fine, darling. Why don't you and your young man join us for breakfast? Ellen's coming, as well, with Penny."

Her gaze locked with David's, Kate barely mumbled an affirmative response before hanging up and springing out of the car.

"You're okay?" she asked when she was wrapped tightly in his embrace. She touched his cheeks, his forehead, his shoulders as if to make sure.

"Keep that up and we're going to cause quite a scene," he taunted lightly.

She lifted her gaze to meet his. "Oh, David, I was so worried about you. When I thought I might never see you again, I wanted to die."

He touched her lips with a finger. "Don't ever, *ever* say that." He held her even more tightly, his own expression mirroring her relief. "I went nuts when I couldn't reach you. Davey even had the car phone number and we tried calling that." He gave her a quelling look. "Even though I knew only a damn fool would be out traipsing around at six in the morning after an earthquake."

She ignored the criticism. "Davey's okay?"

"He's over there with a fireman. What do you think?"

She glanced across the road and saw Davey asking questions of the fireman at a clip that had put a smile on that exhausted face. Her heart filled to overflowing.

"Kate?"

"Umm," she murmured, content to be held.

"I heard what you said on the phone."

She glanced up and met his gaze. "That I love you?"

He nodded. "Did you mean it?"

There was no point in hiding the truth any longer. For better or worse, she loved him. It was time to take a risk. "Have you ever known me to say anything I didn't mean?"

"Enough to marry me?"

A joy unlike anything she had ever experienced before spread through her, sneaking up on her and bringing with it an undeniable sense of fulfillment, but still she was cautious.

"Marriage?"

He tilted her face up. "I love you, Kate," he said with slow emphasis. "Just you."

She wanted so badly to believe. "Are you sure?"

"Absolutely sure. You've made me feel alive again. You've given me back my son. Married or not, we're a family, Kate, in every sense of the word."

She knew that was true. She'd felt it herself for weeks now. She searched his eyes and for the first time there were no shadows, only hope and joy. "Yes," she said then. "Yes, I will marry you."

He swung her off her feet with a cry of such absolute delight that people all along the road turned to stare and smile. Davey came charging across the street.

"Did you ask her, Dad? Did you ask her to marry you?"

David winked at Kate. "I did."

"And did she say yes?" he asked, bouncing up and down with excitement. "She did, didn't she?"

"I did," Kate confirmed.

"All right!" Davey shouted, hugging Kate around the middle.

"We're getting married," he announced to all the observers.

In a morning bleak with destruction and marred by fear, the news was greeted with applause.

"If total strangers are this pleased, just imagine how my family will feel," she said wryly. "Which reminds me, we've been invited to a family breakfast. Are you up to it?"

David brushed a strand of hair from her face and grinned, his hand lingering to cup her chin. "I thought you'd never ask."

When Kate and David pulled up in front of the house she'd grown up in, she looked at the spill of fuchsia bougainvillae, the Spanish tiled roof, the neat lawn, and thought of all the years she'd thought of this house as home. She glanced up at David, caught his smile and felt his hand envelop hers.

"Second thoughts?" he asked.

She shook her head. "Not a one. I was just thinking about what it takes to make a home."

"Two people who love each other," he said. "A family."

"It's taken me a long time to understand that."

"Maybe what's taken a long time was finding the right man to make that happen," he suggested with a devilish twinkle in his eyes.

If he'd expected her to argue, even mildly, she couldn't. There was only one right man for her, and he had taken an impossibly long time to turn up. Or perhaps he'd simply waited until he knew the time was right. Any sooner and she might not have been ready for him.

"I think everyone is going to love you," she told him, grinning. "You're so self-confident."

"Can't see my knees shaking, huh?"

"What are you guys talking about?" Davey demanded. "I'm starved."

"Well, go inside and tell the first person you see to feed you," Kate suggested with a laugh.

Davey's eyes widened. "I can't do that." He glanced at his father. "Can I?"

David chuckled. "No, I suppose not. Come on, Kate, there's no sense putting this off."

"You realize that you have forestalled a lot of problems by making an honest woman of me before our arrival. Otherwise, you could have forgotten having a nice leisurely breakfast with my clan. They'd have been plaguing you with questions."

The possibility didn't seem to concern him. "Kate, you're dallying."

She grinned. "Yes, I guess I am." She took a deep breath. "Let's do it."

By then her mother already had the door open and her arms held wide. "Darling, it's so good to see you. I'm so glad to see for myself that you're okay." She turned her worried expression on David and Davey. "Now, what about you two? Are you okay? Kate told me about the fires."

"We're a little the worse for wear, but nothing serious," David told her. "I'm David Winthrop."

"Well, of course. I've been hearing all about you."

Kate could practically hear alarm bells clanging. She looked up just in time to see Brandon Halloran making his way to the door, his smile warm, his eyes filled with concern as he looked them over.

"David," he said, shaking his hand. "Good to see you again."

"Again?" Kate murmured, looking from one to the other for an explanation. David just smiled. Brandon avoided her gaze altogether. She tugged on David's sleeve. "What does that mean? Again?"

"I'll explain later," he said, just as Ellen swooped in for an introduction, followed by Penny.

"I wish my husband could be here to meet you, too," she said. "He got called in to work." She gave Kate a smug, sisterly look, linked her arm through David's and led him away.

Kate glanced down at Davey. "Let's sneak into the kitchen and see what's cooking."

"Yeah!" he agreed.

Kate found her mother at the stove taking up the last of an entire package of crisp bacon. She sniffed the air appreciatively.

"Should Brandon be eating this?" Kate teased as she saw the bowl of eggs waiting to be scrambled.

"I indulge him once a week," her mother said. "And today is definitely a special occasion."

"Should I be taking notes on how to maintain marital bliss?" Kate inquired idly after she'd sent Davey off with a covered plate of warm biscuits.

Her mother's sharp gaze took in Kate's expression. Suddenly she was laughing and her arms were around Kate. "Oh, darling, I'm so happy for you. He seems like a fine young man."

"Is that the judgment you formed in the last five minutes or has Brandon been indulging in a little more background checking?"

"I believe they had lunch one day last week," her mother admitted.

"They what!"

"Now, dear, we just wanted to be sure that this was the right young man for you."

Davey, back again and clearly bored with the grown-up talk, finally chimed in. "Are we ever going to eat?"

Kate and her mother laughed at his impatience. "In five minutes," Elizabeth Halloran promised her new grandson-to-be. "Why don't you go and tell every-one?"

When everyone was gathered around the dining room table, Brandon glanced down the length of it until his gaze caught with his new wife's. "I think this calls for a blessing, don't you?"

Eyes shining with love, Elizabeth Halloran nodded. The pure happiness on her face brought tears to Kate's eyes.

"Heavenly Father," Brandon began, "thank you for sparing us from today's earthquake and for bringing us all together here this morning. I thank you, too, for my new daughters, my granddaughter and for the fine young man and his son who have brought so much happiness into Kate's life. We ask your blessing on this food we are about to eat and on this family. May we always remember the importance of the love we share. Amen."

Kate lifted her head and looked around the table. At last her glance settled, first on Davey, seated across from her, and then on David at her side. "Amen," she echoed softly.

Beneath the table she felt David's hand reach for hers and close around it. She looked up into eyes that were filled with the radiance of love. Surely they shone no more brightly than her own.

A smile stole across her face. "Now," she said sweetly, "tell me all about this lunch you had with Brandon."

Epilogue

The glass walls and ceiling of the Wayfarer's Chapel high above the Pacific allowed sunlight to spill in on the small group gathered for the wedding of Kate Newton to David Allen Winthrop II. Her heart in her throat, Kate stood on the stone steps at the back of the church and waited for David to take his place before the altar.

Then she turned and smiled at Ellen. "I guess this is it."

"I guess so, little sister." Ellen kissed her cheek. "I love you and I know you're going to be very, very happy."

"Yes," Kate agreed with certainty. "Yes, I am."

"Ladies," Brandon Halloran said, gazing at them

both with eyes filled with tenderness and unmistakably genuine caring. "I believe we're on."

Kate looked up at this white-haired man who had twice blessed her mother's life with happiness. No longer a stranger, once Kate had opened her heart to him, she recognized at last that he was someone she could trust to be there for her, just as her own father once had been.

"Brandon?"

"Yes, my dear."

"Thank you for agreeing to give me away."

"Nothing could have pleased me more than your asking," he said, patting her hand and then linking her arm through his. Kind eyes studied her intently. "All set?"

"Just one more thing. For a time I couldn't imagine how you could care for me the same way you care for Ellen. Then I met Davey, and I couldn't possibly love him any more if he were my own, just because he's David's."

His smile was gentle. "That's the power of love. It has no limitations, my dear. Now, are you ready to begin this new life of yours?"

She took a look down the aisle and let her gaze rest on David and Davey. "Absolutely," she said firmly.

Like her mother just a few months earlier, she couldn't keep the spring out of her step as she closed the gap between herself and the man who'd brought joy into her life and the boy responsible for bringing them together. She glanced up and caught the look that passed between her new stepfather and her mother, saw the tears shimmering on her mother's cheeks.

And then her hand was in David's and the ceremony was underway.

"I, David, take thee, Kate, a woman who has brought new joy into my life, to be my lawfully wedded wife. I give thanks for the day I met you. I love you for your spirit, your generosity and the power of your love, which encompasses not only me, but my son. Together I know we can defeat any obstacle, meet any challenge. I want to grow old with you by my side, and I vow that nothing will ever be more important to me than our family."

Her eyes stinging with unshed tears, Kate met his gaze. For her there was no one else in this wonderful chapel but the man who stood beside her and the God above who would bless their union.

"I, Kate, take thee, David, to be my lawfully wedded husband. Through you I have learned what matters in life. Through you I have discovered the importance of listening to my heart. I know that nothing matters more to me than your happiness and that of our family. When I look into the future, I see you by my side, sharing your strength, your commitment and your love. I vow that whatever obstacles we face, whatever challenges we must meet, we will do so together. You have my respect, and above all, you have my love."

At Kate's insistence there had been no mention of death in the ceremony. She wanted no sad reminders that love didn't always last forever. No one knew that better than David. They would concentrate on the days they had. They would make each one precious, as if it might be their last together. If they succeeded at that, if they cherished each day, when the end of their time on this earth came, they would have no regrets.

Their individual vows spoken and their hands clasped, they looked deep into each other's eyes and echoed the vows spoken at Elizabeth Newton's wedding to Brandon Halloran and at marriage ceremonies throughout time.

They began in a halting cadence, but by the end their voices soared, filling the tiny chapel with their joy. "I promise to love, honor and cherish you all the days of my life."

Outside the chapel on the slope of lawn facing the sea, Kate and David shared a toast with their guests. Because they had planned the wedding in just days, taking the first available date at the chapel, they had kept the guest list small. In a month, when they returned from their honeymoon—the first holiday either had taken in too many years, they would hold a huge reception.

For now, though, Kate was content to be sharing the occasion with family and a handful of people who had seen them both through rough times. She stood amidst the small cluster of well-wishers and felt her heart overflowing with happiness.

Davey came up just then, his expression serious. "Kate?"

"What?" she asked, smiling at him as she thought of what Mrs. Larsen would have to say about his shirttail hanging out and the streak of dirt on the pant leg of his tuxedo. She thought he looked wonderful.

"Should I still call you Kate, now that you and Dad are married?"

Kate's heartbeat stilled, then picked up. *Let me get this right,* she prayed. "What would you like to call me?"

"I was thinking," he began, glancing around until he located his father. "I was thinking that someday, maybe not right away or anything, but someday I'd like to call you Mom."

Kate blinked hard to keep her tears from spilling down her cheeks. "Oh, Davey, I would like that very much, whenever you're ready. Until then, Kate's just fine."

He grinned. "Thanks. Can I go have another piece of cake?"

"You can have all the cake you want."

Just then David's hands settled on her shoulders. "Sure," he teased. "You can tell him that. You're not the one who'll be up with him half the night when his stomach aches."

"Mrs. Larsen won't mind," Kate said with conviction. "She loves him, you know."

"What I know, Kate Newton Winthrop, is that I love you very much and I am ready to get this honeymoon underway."

She pivoted and grinned up at him. "Me, too. Where are we going?"

"That's a secret."

"Somebody has to know." She glanced around. "Dorothy?"

His smug smile told her nothing.

"Zelda?"

Nothing.

"Brandon?"

"What makes you think I've told anybody? Maybe I want complete and total privacy for the next four weeks."

"Now that you mention it, that doesn't sound like such a bad idea."

"Sure you won't miss all the meetings and all the phone calls?"

"Are you sure you won't wish you were in some futuristic kingdom?"

"I guess we'll just have to stay very busy," he taunted.

"Very busy," she agreed. "I have some ideas."

He grinned. "I'll just bet you do. Now how about throwing that bouquet of yours, so we can get this show on the road?"

Kate sent Davey to round up the guests for the ceremonial toss. She stood on the bottom step, took one last peek over her shoulder, then tossed the bouquet into the air. Even without looking, she recognized the squeal of absolute delight.

She turned and walked back to Zelda and gave the redhead a hug, then linked Zelda's arm through hers. "Come on. There's somebody here I definitely want you to meet."

Laughing, they crossed the lawn together until they were in front of Brandon Halloran. Kate winked at him, gestured toward the bouquet clutched tightly in Zelda's hands and said, "Okay, do your thing."

Then she looked around for her husband and her stepson. Her family. When she found them at last, a sigh shimmered through her. It might have taken a long time for her to come to this moment, but she wouldn't have traded the adventure that lay ahead for anything.

* * * * *

A Note From The Author

These times present an exciting challenge for women. As we learn to balance professional and personal lives, just as Kate Newton does in *Kate's Vow*, we open ourselves to a glorious realm of possibilities. Not all of the decisions we make will be easy. Nor will all be free from heartache. We have, however, the opportunity to choose our own futures, to be whatever we want to be—career woman or parent; married or single; or an idyllic, if difficult, combination blending marriage, children *and* a career. That is the choice Kate ultimately, happily makes. Writing *Kate's Vow* as part of Silhouette Books' *That Special Woman* series has given me a wonderful opportunity to celebrate the strengths of all women. We are special because of what we bring openly and enthusiastically to our relationships with men, with children, with each other. Most women, like Kate, possess a unique generosity of spirit, an optimistic view of the world that encompasses joy, compassion and hope. In the end, what makes Kate special is what makes each of us special— a will to learn and grow, a determination to survive, a deep understanding of the value of friendship and, most of all, an unstinting capacity to love. I wish that for each of you, along with a very special man with whom to share them.

Fifty red-blooded, white-hot, true-blue hunks from every State in the Union!

Beginning in May, look for MEN MADE IN AMERICA! Written by some of our most popular authors, these stories feature fifty of the strongest, sexiest men, each from a different state in the union!

Two titles available every other month at your favorite retail outlet.

In July, look for:

CALL IT DESTINY by Jayne Ann Krentz (Arizona)
ANOTHER KIND OF LOVE by Mary Lynn Baxter (Arkansas)

In September, look for:

DECEPTIONS by Annette Broadrick (California)
STORMWALKER by Dallas Schulze (Colorado)

You won't be able to resist MEN MADE IN AMERICA!

SILHOUETTE SPECIAL EDITION®

MORGAN'S MERCENARIES

by
Lindsay McKenna

Morgan Trayhern has returned and he's set up a company full of best pals in adventure. Three men who've been to hell and back are about to fight the toughest battle of all . . . love!

You loved Wolf Harding in HEART OF THE WOLF (SE #818), so be sure to catch the other two stories in this exciting trilogy.
Sean Killian a.k.a. THE ROGUE (SE #824) is coming your way in July.
And in August it's COMMANDO (SE #830) with hero Jake Randolph.

These are men you'll love and stories you'll treasure . . . only from Silhouette Special Edition!

Silhouette

SPECIAL EDITION

From this day forward

**Coming in August,
the first book in an exciting new trilogy from
Debbie Macomber
GROOM WANTED**

To save the family business, Julia Conrad becomes a "green card" bride to brilliant chemist Aleksandr Berinski. But what more would it take to keep her prized employee—and new husband—happy?

FROM THIS DAY FORWARD—Three couples marry first and find love later in this heartwarming trilogy.

**Look for
Bride Wanted (SE #836) in September
Marriage Wanted (SE #842) in October**

Only from Silhouette Special Edition